UNCHARTED TERRITORY

STONECROFT SAGA 6

B.N. RUNDELL

WOLFPACK
PUBLISHING
····· EST 2010 ·····

WOLFPACK
PUBLISHING
— EST 2013 —

Uncharted Territory

Paperback Edition
Copyright © 2020 B.N. Rundell

Wolfpack Publishing
6032 Wheat Penny Avenue
Las Vegas, NV 89122

wolfpackpublishing.com

Paperback ISBN 978-1-64734-501-3
eBook ISBN 978-1-64734-500-6

UNCHARTED TERRITORY

Dedication

To my readers . . . Enjoy the ride!

1 / West

He cast a long shadow. Broad shoulders over a six-foot frame that strained at the weathered buckskins, dusty blonde wavy hair that covered his collar, a floppy felt hat that shaded his eyes and trimmed whiskers, while piercing green eyes glared from under his brow. Dark tanned skin showed at the ends of fringed sleeves and beaded toed moccasins rested in the stirrups of the Dragoon saddle. His long-legged black Andalusian stallion stretched out with strides that covered the rugged ground of the northern plains. Gabe Stone was also known as Spirit Bear or Bear Claw by many of the native peoples and had become a familiar figure in the uncharted territory of the north country. He believed in always being prepared and well-armed, carrying a rare Ferguson breech loading rifle, a matched pair of over/under double barreled French saddle pistols, a Bailes turnover double barreled belt pistol, a pair of custom-made Flemish knives that hung between his shoulder blades, a tomahawk at his belt, and a Mongol bow in a case beneath his left leg. This arsenal had been chosen from his father's extensive collection and Gabe was exceptionally skilled with each weapon.

His constant companion, Ezra Blackwell, a solid built man that referred to himself as Black Irish, after his Black Irish mother, had ridden with him since they left Philadelphia, with bounty hunters on their trail after Gabriel Stonecroft had killed the son of a prominent member of the Second Continental Congress. Although it was an honest duel and fought according to the rules of the *Co·e Duello*, old man Wilson vowed to find his vengeance by placing a significant bounty on young Stonecroft's head, and the two life-long friends left the east, knowing they would be exiled for life. And while Gabe was well armed, Ezra had also been outfitted quite well. He carried a Lancaster style long rifle, a duplicate of Gabe's over/under Bailes pistol, a hawk, knife and added an exceptionally crafted war club in the shape of a rifle stock and made from the root of an ironwood tree. It was decorated by inlaid stones, held a Halberd blade half buried in the root ball at its head. This had become his weapon of choice in close-up combat and he had become very skilled and deadly with its use.

Ezra's father was a pastor of the largest African Methodist Episcopal church in Philadelphia and knew the two friends were inseparable when he bid his only son goodbye, perhaps forever. But he had known this time would come as the men had dreamed of exploring the western wilderness known as French Louisiana since they were children that roamed the forests at every opportunity.

The men had traveled down the Ohio River from Pittsburg aboard a flatboat, taken to the wilderness after crossing the Mississippi, and had become friends with many different native peoples. But when they met two sisters among the Shoshone, the men had grown tired of the lonely life and now, no longer single, they traveled with their wives, Pale Otter and Grey Dove. It was their fourth year in the wilderness of the west and what they had seen only whetted their appetite for more. It was that wanderlust and insatiable passion to discover and explore that set them on this trail.

They had been traveling west for the last week, anxious to put behind them the events of the previous weeks when the women and Ezra had been taken by the renegade French Coureur des bois and his band, who had been intent on selling them into slavery, until Gabe was practically resurrected from the dead and came to their deliverance. Originally intent on following the Rocky Mountain range to the north, their little detour had been both time-consuming and life threatening, an experience they were anxious to put behind them.

Gabe reined up on the east bank of the river that would one day be known as the Clark's Fork, but was now known as the South Fork of the *Roche Jaune* or Yellow Rock or the Elk River as it was known by the Crow people. The banks of the river were lined with willow, alder, chokecherry bushes, and cottonwood trees. As near as he could tell the river was about a hundred feet across, but the gravelly bottom showed through the clear water and the easy moving current appeared to be crossable and not more than three or four feet deep. He looked at the others and Ezra said, "Don't look too bad to me. I think we could cross it here 'bout as good as anywhere."

Otter glanced at her husband and with one of her mischievous grins, gigged her blue roan gelding into the water as she dragged the steeldust mustang pack horse behind her. Gabe shook his head and kneed his big black to follow, jerking on the lead line of the little sorrel pack horse to bring her along. Ezra motioned for Grey Dove to follow, and he brought up the rear as he led the grulla mare pack horse. It was an easy and uneventful crossing, and each one stepped down to allow the horses to give a rolling shake to rid themselves of the water that clung to their bellies and legs.

Ezra lifted his eyes to the sun, looked back to Gabe, grinned, "I think we oughta take a break and have us some o' the leftovers from this mornin'. After all, we need to do what we can to lighten the loads of them pack horses, don'tcha think?"

Gabe looked at his friend, grinned and shook his head, "And you see it as your duty to help out those poor tired packhorses, don't you?"

"Yup, just tryin' to be a help!" he answered as he turned to the parfleche that held the foodstuffs. Gabe started loosening the girth on his saddle, then went to each of the other animals and did likewise, giving the horses a little relief and to let them graze on the tall grass on the riverbank.

The women took over the task of fixing the meal, making a small smokeless fire with the dried and grey sticks from the cottonwoods and setting out the johnny cakes on the rock close to the fire, then hanging the strip steaks on the willow withes to suspend them over the fire. At the feet of Otter lay a big black wolf, known affectionately as Wolf, a constant companion of the woman since he was found as a three-week old pup in a cave behind their cabin. Ezra went to Gabe's side and watched as he dug out the brass telescope from his saddlebags. "Gonna reconnoiter a little are ya?" he asked.

Gabe grinned, nodding his head, and motioned to the many ridges that rose between the ravines and gullies carved by runoff from the snow melt and the frequent spring showers. "Those ridges there'll be good high ground for a look see."

"The buffalo are gettin' more numerous, and the

herds are bigger. I'm thinkin' we're not too far behind the big migrating herd," responded Ezra. Both men knew he implied that with the abundance of buffalo the chances of meeting up with native hunting parties were increasing. They were still in Crow country, and they had made peace with a few bands of both the mountain Crow and the river Crow. But they were nearing the land of the Blackfoot and the Flathead, and both people were known to come from their homes in the mountains and make extended hunts in the plains for the migrating buffalo herds. And the last they heard was that both tribes were not too friendly with any newcomers to their territory.

Gabe shinnied up the loose adobe clay soil to the top of the ridge that stood about a hundred feet above their makeshift camp by the river. Once atop he sat down, stretched out the scope and with both elbows on his knees, he began to scan the countryside. Ezra sat beside him, watching, and asked, "Anythin' interestin'?"

"Ummm," grunted Gabe, moving the scope slowly along the far ridges. "This valley here leads all the way to that far ridge yonder, 'bout eight or nine miles, then they top out into a big flat." He paused a few moments, still moving the scope, "And down here in that valley there's a little bunch of buffalo, maybe we can get us some fresh meat." He moved, paused, moved again, and finally, "Other'n that, just a few antelope, deer, a couple coyotes, and a whole lotta mighty big country."

He lowered the scope, offered it to Ezra and wrapped his arms around his knees, looking around at the nearby territory. The green valley of the river behind him stretched out to the north, having carved its way through the desolate landscape of sage brush, creosote, grease wood, and cacti to make its rendez-vous with the distant Yellowstone and on to the Missouri. The hilly and rolling terrain stretched beyond his vision, marred by ridges, plateaus, ravines and uplifts. It was a fascinating country inhabited by many different native peoples and a land seen only by some French traders and trappers of the Hudson's Bay or Northwest Companies, ancient excursions by Spanish Conquistadors, and a very few Americans. But it was a land that could swallow up the entire population of the newfound United States of America, and still have millions of acres of uninhabited territory.

Gabe and Ezra were continually amazed at the wonders and the vastness of this wilderness, and every day they made new discoveries that caused them to look heavenward and praise the mighty Creator for his workmanship. Ezra finished his scan, handed the scope back to his friend and said, "I'm hungry." And when Ezra was hungry, there was no sense trying to talk about anything else or do anything but feed the man. Gabe looked at his friend, grinned, and shook his head as he cased the scope and stood to slide down the slope of the ridge, digging in their heels to slow their descent and once down, trotted to the women's side.

***

By late afternoon, they were approaching the head-waters of the little creek that lay in the bottom of the long valley viewed from the ridge at the last stop. The sides of the valley now crowded in, holding an abundance of piñon and juniper on the east facing slope, yet bare on the west slopes. The game trail that followed the creek in the bottom, crossed and re-crossed the chuckling stream, weaving in and out of the chokecherries and willows. The wary buffalo had ambled ahead of them, never letting the small group get within shooting range and when the valley narrowed, Gabe chose to let up and give the bison room to find themselves a place to bed down. As they came to the head of the valley, the stream bed was a narrow cascade of tumbling water that came from the flats above. Gabe nodded toward a small basin that lay surrounded by cottonwood and juniper that offered protection and cover for a good campsite.

They stripped the gear from the packhorses and the women's mounts, tethering them within reach of both water and graze, then Gabe stepped beside Otter, "We're goin' up on the hills yonder, have a look-see and maybe get us some fresh meat."

Otter smiled at her man, gently lay her hand on his

chest as she looked up at him, "We," nodding toward her sister, Grey Dove, "will go to that pool in the bottom and wash. It has been a long dry day and we are very dusty. But if you want to join us . . .?" she smiled up at him coyly.

Gabe chuckled, "That is tempting, but, we need the meat and we might be able to get us a buffalo."

"Alright then, we'll be ready when you come back. Should we have a fire and meat on to cook?"

Gabe grinned, drew her close, "No, we'll bring some fresh meat and have nice steaks to cook and meat to smoke. So, we'll have a day or two here to take advantage of that pool yonder."

Otter grinned at her man, pushed him back and said, "Then you better get to huntin'."

***

They rode from the narrow defile and over a long low hill, then dropped into a wide green basin that lay in the shadow of a long round-top ridge. They tethered their horses beside a cluster of piñon and walked to the top of the ridge. The bald top offered nothing in the way of cover and both men bellied down to use the bunch grass to shield their presence. Ezra pointed to the west and a wide green flat that seemed to be the long skirt of the mountain range that rose high above. The flatlands were a smattering of green and brown, but the brown slowly moved like a continuous wave as the grass blown in the wind. Both men recognized the massive herd of buffalo slowly thinning out, lazily grazing and some already bedding down. Gabe grinned at Ezra as he slid the scope from its case and stretched it out for a close look at the vast herd.

The wind shifted and came from the north, bringing the thunderous bellows and grunts, rattle of horns, and shuffling of millions of hooves, as the herd milled about, interspersed with the twitter and whistle of the buffalo birds. It also carried the unmistakable smell of buffalo, urine, feces, dust, and more. As he watched, several were rolling in the dirt, coating themselves with a layer of dust that would serve as protection against parasites.

Gabe turned to Ezra, "I don't think they've been there long. They'll probably spread out and graze for several days, lots of tall grass there and plenty of water. But right down below us here is a small bunch that musta broke off from 'em." He pointed with his chin as he spoke, and Ezra lifted up to see the wooly boogers.

"There's a young bull and a couple nice cows in that little bunch, make good eatin' and they ain't got no calves with 'em."

"Ummhmmm," answered Gabe, grinning as he put the scope in the case. "But, I think I'll use my bow, just in case there's some un-friendlies around."

2 / Buffalo

The Mongol bow that was Gabe's preferred weapon for hunting had both made him into the man he was and improved his every skill as a hunter. With a draw weight of well over a hundred pounds, the young Gabe refused to be overcome by the bow and daily worked at becoming the master of the medieval weapon. His shoulders, back and arms gained muscle, his fingers became calloused, and his patience was melded with his skill so that he had mastered the weapon by his late teens. He had been driven as much by his stubborn competitiveness as he was by the ballads and books he had read as a youth about the legend of the forest, Robin Hood. When Gabe and his father made their trip to England and Europe in his early teens, they saw the Shakespearean play *The Two Gentlemen of Verona* where the outlaws said, "By the bare scalp of Robin Hood's fat friar, this fellow were a king for our wild faction!" which inspired the young man to read everything he could find about the character, Robin Hood, and was subsequently stirred to emulate the legend. Upon his return to the forests around Philadelphia, he and his friend, Ezra, often played the parts of Robin Hood and Little John and battled one another with quarterstaffs. Gabe remembered a time that Ezra wanted to be Friar Tuck, but was quickly discouraged when Gabe said, "Friar Tuck was a preacher like your father, but Little John was a fighter!" And although Ezra's father was a pastor, he had no inclination to be like him.

The Mongol bow was a laminated recurve weapon with a core of bamboo, the belly layered with the horn of mountain sheep, the outer side with sinew and all bonded with a glue made from the bladders of fresh water fish. The whole was covered with a layer of birch bark to serve as a moisture barrier. As Gabe drew the bow from the leather case, he sat on a flat boulder and used his feet to support the bow, one on either side of the grip, as he drew the limbs back toward his chest to nock the string. He stood, slipped his jade thumb ring on and hung the quiver at his side, and with a nod to Ezra, started his stalk of the buffalo.

Gabe had plotted his stalk from high atop the knoll, where he watched as the big herd of buffalo grazed in the broad flats beyond the stream that came from the northern end of the Absaroka Mountains. That stream was shouldered by a long bald finger ridge that pointed into the flats and extended about five or six miles from the mountain range. But between the ridge and Gabe, was a wide shallow arroyo where the smaller bunch of buffalo grazed. Ezra still lay atop the bald knob they had used to reconnoiter the valley when they spotted the bison below the point, and would signal if the animals moved before he came near. With little cover to shield his approach, Gabe chose to move into the lower end of the brushy arroyo and make his stalk along the trickle of water in the bottom.

From his vantage point atop the knoll, Gabe had seen the small bunch had a mature bull, a young bull, two young cows, a mature cow and a yearling still wearing his orange coat. He preferred to take the young bull, leaving the young cows to someday add to the herd. As he rounded the point of the knoll he went to a crouch and angled away from the animals, moving steadily toward the chokecherry brush beside the little spring fed stream. He dropped down behind the cluster of brush, then moved to get a better sight on the bison. They were about five hundred yards away, lazily grazing near the small pool that lay below the spring. As he looked their direction, he plotted his course through the brush. Beside the creek were chokecherry, some serviceberry, and the smaller kinnikinnick. It would be a difficult stalk, most of it in a crouch or even crawling. While away from the creek bottom, the slopes of the gulley held scattered patches of scrub oak or what most called buck brush, that was taller and thicker and offered better cover, but also more difficult to penetrate.

He looked from the grass to the dry slopes, realizing a stalk in the grass would be wet, but he decided to stay in the bottom of the coulee to make his approach. He stayed in a crouch, crossed the trickle of water and kept what shrubbery, stunted though it was, between him and the animals. He watched as best he could, moving only when the heads of the old bull and cow were turned away or down and grazing, they would be the ones most likely to spook and alarm the others. He moved easily through the damp grass, and within moments had cut the distance to less than two hundred yards. He dropped to one knee, breathed deep to catch his wind and slow his heartbeat, and when properly rested, he slowly raised up to gauge his distance and possible shot. The bunch had moved closer together, and Gabe dropped into his crouch, then to his knees and inched closer. His goal was a serviceberry bush that stood taller than most and sat right at the edge of the stream.

His stop and go progress finally brought him behind the taller brush and within a little less than a hundred yards of the nearest buffalo, the young bull. He steadied himself for a moment, then stealthily rose to one knee and nocked an arrow. He waited another moment, watching the bull munch on the grass and slowly move forward. When the bull had stretched out his neck and foreleg for a fresh bunch of grass, Gabe let the arrow fly. Even before the feathered missile found its mark, he had nocked a second arrow and chose his target.

The bull stumbled with the strike of the arrow that buried itself deep in the lower chest, just behind the front leg, and as he staggered, the second arrow found its mark in the neck of the bull, a handbreadth behind the ear. The bull tried to raise its head, stumbled again, and buried his nose in the grass as he fell forward with a grunt. The other buffalo looked at the fallen beast, the big bull swinging his head side to side and snorting, but it was the old cow that started the bunch moving as she led them away from the gulley and over the ridge toward the rest of the herd. They ambled on their way, unalarmed, but moving away from what they didn't understand.

As the other buffalo disappeared over the ridge, Gabe rose, looking toward the top of the knoll and saw Ezra starting down the slope to help. Gabe knew Ezra would fetch the horses and bring Ebony, his big black stallion, to him. When he came near, Ezra chuckled and said, "I thought that big 'un was gonna charge you!"

Gabe grinned, "I was more concerned with that old cow. I think she spotted me and that's why she moved 'em out. Usually they don't spook, and you can take several before they get too restless, but I guess with the small bunch, she was a little jittery."

"Well, anyway, we've got us some fresh meat and plenty of it!" declared Ezra.

Gabe looked at the downed bull, "I'll start the butcherin' if you'll help me move him around so I can bleed him out."

Ezra looked at the bull that was on its belly, legs stretched out on either side of its head

looking like it was just laying in the grass, but the heavy carcass would need everything both men could do to turn it so the head was slightly downhill, and the carcass would bleed out rather than pool in the meat and spoil. Ezra stepped near, stood in front of the massive head and grabbed the horns, then looked at his friend, "Well, c'mon! I ain't doin' this by myself!"

Gabe chuckled, grabbed the downhill front leg and the two pulled and tugged to get the beast turned. Once finished, both sat on the carcass, breathing deep, and Ezra said, "That's a lotta meat!"

"Ummhmmm, but it's gonna be mighty fine eating!"

Ezra grinned, stood and went to his bay, mounted up and started for the camp. Ezra left and Gabe tethered Ebony to the nearby brush, loosened his girth, and then turned back to his bloody task.

When the women arrived, they, being more experienced and adept, quickly took over the task, including instructing the men in the heavier work. Otter stood, arms bloody to her elbows, and waved the men near, "You two, while we finish cutting through here," pointing to the big neck, "you can pull the hide down then roll him over."

Gabe and Ezra looked at one another, then started to work with their larger knives, cutting away the hide, peeling it down, and tucking it close so they could roll the carcass as instructed. They had finished, stood and stretched, and Dove said, "That pile needs to be drug away, over by that brush," pointing to the gut pile and the oak brush about fifty feet away.

Ezra looked at the offal, then to Gabe, and both men hung their heads and started for the bloody entrails. As they started, they looked up to see the circling turkey buzzards, a lone eagle, and several ravens. Two coyotes were pacing back and forth, and a badger was trotting directly toward them and the pile. Ezra picked up a good-sized stone and chucked it at the low hung striped predator, but the badger kept coming. Gabe tried to discourage it with a rock, to no avail and it kept coming until Otter used her sling and struck the badger on its nose with a rock, turning it aside. Gabe and Ezra looked back at the woman, saw her standing and smiling at the men, then started their assigned task of dragging away the gut pile, all the while making faces at the refuse.

The women kept Wolf close by, tossing him scraps

to keep him away from the gathering bunch of buzzards, badgers and coyotes and other carrion eaters, although Wolf could have made short work of them all.

Dusk was closing the doors on daylight as they led the packhorses back into their camp, but enough light remained for them to hang the quartered buffalo and to start the hard work of preserving the hide and meat as well as the usual chores of the camp. Gabe tended to all the horses, giving each a good rubdown with handfuls of grass, then taking them for a long drink before tethering them near the trees but within reach of graze.

Dove was busy at the fire and looked up as both men came near, "It will be ready soon," pointing to the pot of stew hanging over the fire.

"I'm so hungry my belly button's pinchin' my backbone!" declared Ezra, reaching for a piece of johnny-cake. Otter was fashioning some willow drying racks near the fire, and Ezra wrestled around a sizeable flat rock that would become their cutting table. He sat down on the stone, looked at Wolf, who was sniffing around for any dropped morsels he might find, and asked, "Ain't he had enough to eat?"

Gabe laughed, "He's just like you, always wanting something to eat!"

"Can I help it that I'm just a growin' boy, like my Mama used to say?"

Gabe laughed, "If you're a growing boy, I can't

imagine what you'll be like when you're finally grown!" Both women giggled at the thought, as Ezra feigned hurt feelings.

Gabe sat down to unstring his bow and clean and repair the retrieved arrows, always careful to maintain the metal points and keep them sharp. His arrows were six to nine inches longer than the common arrows used by the natives with their smaller bows and finding the alder or birch that was suitable was not an easy task, so he was careful with what he had, but one of the arrows, the one that struck the neck, was broken and he was measuring it to see if he could use the shorter shaft. But it was split too far, and he salvaged the point and fletching, tossing the shaft into the fire.

They worked into the night, with the light of the fire and moon. Gabe and Ezra cut the meat into the thin strips, while Otter and Dove made the racks, hung the meat, and tended the smoke fires. As they worked, Ezra paused often, looking around at the night, brow furrowed, listening. Gabe asked, "What is it?"

Ezra tried to make light of his feelings, "Oh, prob'ly nothin'."

Yet Gabe was well aware of the gift of precognition that Ezra inherited from his mother and her Black Irish ancestors whose Celtic genealogy included a line of druids in the old country. Although he seldom made mention of it or paid much attention to the unsettled feelings, it had been of benefit before and had, on occasion, spared their lives. After the third time of Ezra's walking off a few steps to look and listen, Gabe asked again, "What is it?"

Ezra walked back to their work, shaking his head, "I dunno. Something's not right, listen." He nodded to the trees and the dark. Nothing stirred, there were no questions from the wise old owls that hunted in the darkness, no cries from circling nighthawks, even the bullfrogs from the bog below had gone quiet. The only sound came from a scuff of a hoof as the horses shifted their weights and the cicadas had also fallen silent.

The men stood still, listening, turning to face a different direction, even cupping their ears. But the darkness had dropped the curtain of silence completely. Gabe looked to Wolf who lay nearby and he rested peacefully with his chin on his paws, eyes closed, and his chest expanding rhythmically. Gabe looked to Ebony. The big stallion stood hipshot, head hanging, unmoving.

"Let's finish this little bit," said Gabe, nodding to the meat that remained on the rock, "and then turn in. I don't think there's any predators about or Indians for that matter." He pointed to Wolf and the horses with his chin, "They're quiet."

Ezra breathed deep, lifting his shoulders, and with another quick glance around, resumed his meat cutting.

***

Gabe and Otter lay staring at the stars for a while, sharing quiet thoughts but soon tired and dozed off. Ezra's muted snoring broke the silence and Dove was heard as she flounced under the covers, trying to get comfortable. Even with a late night, when they turned in there were still two quarters of buffalo hanging in the lone cottonwood. With Wolf and the horses to keep watch, all four were soon deep in sleep for the night.

3 / Thunder

The cold nose of Wolf touched the exposed neck of Gabe, bringing him instantly awake. Gabe looked at the wolf, who sat back on his haunches, staring at the man, then scanned the darkness. Gabe knew if there was danger, Wolf's action would be one of alert and protection, but when Gabe saw movement, he recognized Ezra near the horses. Gabe turned to look at Otter, who was awake and watching, then rolled from his blankets and walked to Ezra's side.

"Goin' somewhere?" asked Gabe, speaking barely above a whisper. Ezra was busy saddling his horse and did not turn to face his friend but answered, "We need to get outta here!" Although the words were whispered, the urgency and alarm were evident. Gabe looked at his friend, then nodded and went to Ebony. Without a word, Otter had touched Dove and both women were beside their men and began saddling their own horses. Within moments, all the horses were geared up, everything was packed and loaded, and Gabe nodded to Ezra, as he mounted up, giving him the go-ahead to lead out.

Ezra led them to the bald knoll the men had used when they spotted the buffalo, but as soon as he crested the hump, the moonlight showed the trail he was searching for and he took it at a canter. The lead rope of the grulla mustang packhorse was stretched tight as Ezra lay along his horse's neck, one arm stiffened behind him, dragging the packhorse. Dove was close behind with Otter leading the steeldust mustang followed by Gabe leading the little sorrel. They stayed with Ezra, and he never slackened the pace, even as the trail dipped off the knoll and rose to the long finger ridge. The bald ridge stretched out in the moonlight, pointing toward the mountain range, and the horses were kicking up dust as they fanned out, none wanting to ride in the dust of the one before them. The seven horses made their own muted thunder on the soft soiled ridge, and if it were daylight, they could be seen for miles. But the darkness seemed to dull the sounds and dim the trail, until another thunder broke loose.

Everyone looked at the sky, expecting to see billowing thunder clouds and lightning, but the black sky was an anomaly. There were no clouds, no lightning, only the blanket of stars that twinkled like diamonds on velvet. Ezra suddenly reined up, swinging a leg over the rump of his bay gelding before the animal slid to a stop. He hollered, "Get down! Now! Hold the horses tight!"

The thunder rolled, but when their feet hit the ground, everyone stumbled, Dove fell on her rump, but held tight to the reins of her buckskin. The horses were wide eyed, legs stiff, as they looked at the ground and swung their heads side to side, panicky, fearful, unknowing. Gabe put his arm around the neck of Ebony, spoke softly to the big stallion, and then reached out for Otter, drawing her close. Both dropped to their knees, looking askance in every direction, the ground moving under them. Gabe's first thought was that the herd of buffalo had stampeded and was coming their way, but there was nothing. When he was shaken again, he realized the ground was moving, and he recognized his first real earthquake.

Otter held tight to the reins and lead rope of the steeldust, then leaned back against Gabe, "What is it? What's happening?" she shouted, with the roar of the thundering ground, the fearful whinnying of the horses, and her own fear rising within, she had to shout to be heard.

"Earthquake!" shouted Gabe, "Earthquake!"

Otter looked at her man, saw he was stoic and standing firm, but fear was not showing. She took comfort in that and sought to muster her own courage and strength. Dove was beside Ezra, both were sitting on the ground, but still holding tight to the horses. When the Grulla tried to rear up and break away, Ezra pulled the horse's head down and stood beside her, stroking her neck and speaking softly into her ear, calming the mare. He reached out and stroked the buckskin, speaking to him as well, then to his bay.

But another thunder seemed to rise, the ground trembled, and they looked to the flats that stretched north from the mountains to see the brown blanket of buffalo on the move. Thousands of woolies moved as one, thundering eastward toward the thin grey line of early morning. One star remained in the eastern sky, a lone signal lantern that seemed to beckon and promise deliverance. The herd rumbled toward the end of the long ridge, rising up and over it like a tidal wave from the ocean, sweeping under everything in its path. The vibration of the ground was different, the rumble of the stampeding beasts felt beneath them, but the ground did not move as before.

The bellowing, grunting, bawling of the thousands of bison was a discordant symphony that echoed back from the mountains behind them, driving them onward. The earthquake had frightened them, but the thunderous stampede would frighten any living thing in its path and death and destruction would leave a wide trail. The tide of turmoil seemed endless as the small band of explorers watched, long shadows of early morning stretching out behind the beasts as they charged into the rising sun.

It had taken months for the migration of bison to bring this massive herd to the north country, and now if they did not slow their flight, the many tribes of native peoples would face a dire winter. Without ample stores of meat, hides for shelter and clothing, bones and sinew for tools and more, many would die. They depended on the buffalo for most everything they used and needed and without the bounty from successful hunts, desolation lay on the horizon.

Gabe and company had settled the horses down, and now sat together watching the stragglers of the big herd follow the turned-up trail made by the passing of the wooly beasts. As the sunlight splashed on the east facing slopes of the mountains, they saw the trails and dust of many rockslides where massive chunks of rock had broken from granite faced cliffs and tumbled down, plowing a channel of destruction before them and leaving paths of flattened forests and broken boulders. All across the mountains, puffs and pillars of dust rose into the morning sky, each one telling the story of destruction and the re-shaping of mountain faces.

As they looked down the slope of the long ridge, what had been a smooth, almost groomed slope, now showed deep dimples of sunken ground and humps of heaved soil, making the long slope appear as a wrinkled blanket, rumpled by a late sleeper and left askew. Gabe pointed to the creek below, "Look at that!"

Otter craned around to see what he was pointing out, "You mean that stream?"

"Yeah, look, the ground cracked open and the stream disappears!"

Otter's eyes flared and she put a hand to her mouth as she leaned forward to look again. She searched the creek bottom, then pointed, "There! It comes up again!" About sixty yards further down the creek bottom, the stream sparkled in the sunlight, but was now wide spread and nowhere near its original bed.

Ezra stood and looked back down the trail, "Take a gander at that," he said, pointing with his chin.

Everyone turned and looked where he indicated, each one slowly stood and stared. Where they had camped, was now nothing but churned soil where the stampede had passed. Had they stayed, they could have been trampled or at the least, lost much of their gear and perhaps their horses, but most likely everything would have been lost. Each one turned in his own time to look at Ezra, wondering, until Otter asked, "How did you know?"

Ezra dropped his eyes, poked at a rock with his toe, then looked up, "I dunno. It just happens sometime, I don't know exactly, but it just seems to take over and unless I do whatever it is, I just don't have any peace about anything."

"He had noticed the silence of the night, told me about it," added Gabe. "He's done that before, so I know better than to question him."

The women looked at him and Dove said, "Even the most powerful shaman cannot do that. If you were among our people, you would be a shaman."

Otter nodded, then Ezra responded. "It's something that comes from my mother. Her people were that way, back in the old country. Not everyone, mind you, just our family."

Gabe turned and looked back toward the mountains, "Look's like somebody else was after the buffalo," and nodded toward the edge of the flats. He turned back to his saddle bags and withdrew the scope, dropped to one knee and stretched it out. "Look like Blackfoot."

Ezra said, "What about these over here?" he pointed to the valley that held the creek below them. The valley split the mountains and bent around the back of one, but at its mouth and below where Gabe and company now stood, was a band of ten or twelve warriors, riding slowly toward the churned ground left behind by the buffalo.

Gabe swung back and looked at the larger group, "Dunno." He looked to Otter, handed her the scope and waited.

"Agaidika, or Bannock," stated Otter, lowering the scope.

4 / Visitors

Gabe looked at Otter, "Those two tribes," nodding toward those below and to the smaller band beyond, "enemies?"

"Sometimes, but when they are on a hunt, most do not fight each other. But we are in Crow land and if they follow the buffalo, they will be considered invaders," explained Otter, looking from one group to the other. "These," nodding to those below them, "are Northern Shoshone."

Gabe looked at Otter, frowning, "They're your people?"

Otter smiled, "My people are the *Kuccuntikka*, or buffalo eaters. These are the *Agaideka*, or salmon eaters. The Bannock are friends with the Shoshone and often take wives from the *Agaideka* and our people take wives from the Bannock."

As they spoke, they watched the band in the valley below to see the group stop and one of the warriors motioning toward them. Although they were high on the long ridge that shouldered the valley, they were in the open and easily seen. Gabe said, "They've seen us."

While they watched, five warriors broke off from the larger band and started up the slope toward them at a canter. Gabe looked at Otter, "You're sure they're friendly?"

Otter grinned, "I will speak with them," and moved away from the rest, toward the approaching warriors. She held up one hand, palm toward them, and spoke to the leader. Gabe, Ezra and Dove listened as Otter introduced herself, motioned toward them and gave their names. The leader, an Agaidika, spoke in Shoshone and said, "I am Shoots Running Buffalo, he," nodding to the warrior beside him, "is Sitting Turtle. Why are you here, is this not the land of the Apsáalooke?"

"Yes, this is Crow land, and we have fought and made peace with some of the Crow people. But we are going into the land of the Blackfoot and Salish."

The leader frowned, "Do these men wish to die?" he asked, pointing toward Gabe and Ezra.

Otter grinned, "My man and his friend are great warriors! They have fought against many, but we do not go to fight, but to explore the new lands, and to make peace with others."

Shoots Running Buffalo frowned, shrugged, "Did you see the Nimerigar that made the mountains move?" He spoke of the legendary magical race of violent little people that battled the Shoshone people from underground.

"No, and my man says when the ground moves and shakes like that it is called an earthquake and is common in other lands. He also says it is normal for it to happen again soon, but it will not be as bad."

"Is your man a *boha grande?*" meaning a shaman.

Otter grinned, "No, but his friend told us about the moving of the earth before it happened so we could move our camp and be safe. He can see things like that."

Shoots frowned, glanced toward Ezra and leaned down and scowled at Otter, speaking just above a whisper, "But, he looks like a *bozheena!*"

"That is why he is called Black Buffalo."

Shoots sat up, nodded toward the band below, "With the buffalo gone, we will return to our people. You may come, if you want. Our village is two days," pointing into the mountain valley that carried the creek below.

The off handed invitation made Otter grin and turn away. She walked back to Gabe and said, "We have been invited to return to their village with them. It is an honor."

"Where is their village?" asked Gabe.

"Two days into that valley, and I believe they are near the Yellowstone River."

Gabe looked at Ezra and Dove, then back at Otter. "I reckon." He saw both Ezra and the women smile at his response, accepting his decision as a good one.

***

The leader of the band of warriors was *Owitze*, Twisted Hand, a Tussawehee White Knife dog soldier, and when Gabe and company came to the band, he nodded an acknowledgment when they were introduced, glanced at the big wolf at their feet, looked back at Gabe then motioned to his warriors to follow as they turned to go back up the valley into the mountains. Gabe and company followed a short way behind, staying to themselves.

As they started into the mountains, massive granite tipped peaks seemed to shoulder in and narrow the valley. The stream in the bottom was bordered with willows, alder, and berry bushes, while small patches of grass carpeted the valley bottom. Wherever they looked, there was evidence of the earthquake, with trees toppled, boulders and rockslides, and in the bottom the creek had repeatedly jumped its banks as the ground heaved earthen dams in its way. The trail rode the bottom of the long steep sloping and heavily timbered shoulder on their left and across the creek the limestone rose over two thousand feet almost straight up to dwarf the riders in the bottom, yet even here the damage was seen. A huge slice of limestone had slid away from the cliff-face and tumbled into a heap at its base, broken shards the size of a small cabin lay askew as if thrown from high above and driven into the ground.

When the creek bottom bent around the limestone cliffs, several timbered monoliths stood as sentinels guarding the passageway below. They rode southwest into the canyon until it turned due west. The flat-bottomed gorge spanned about three to four hundred yards but the further upstream they traveled the mountains slowly crowded in on them. They had ridden about seven or eight miles when the canyon bent again to the south. A side canyon echoed with the sound of cascading water and the leader turned into the trees to follow the narrow stream.

They soon broke into a clearing that held a small pond with grassy banks, fed by a narrow waterfall dropping white water from a height of about a hundred feet, but the captivating sight that froze all the riders was a massive silver-tip grizzly bear, splashing in the water, obviously fishing for its dinner. When the leader reined up, he held up his hand to the others, and each one sat immobile, looking at the huge boar. Suddenly the bear caught their scent and stood on his hind feet, water barely to his knees, as he towered over the pool of water, now dwarfed by his size. He cocked his head to the side, his small black eyes glaring at the intruders and he led out a roar that echoed across the narrow canyon, startling the horses and instantly pandemonium razed the canyon, horses bucking, men grabbing at manes, reins, and anything to try to stay aboard the frightened horses as they bucked and kicked, trying to escape from the tiny clearing. But with so many riders, the trail was blocked by Gabe and friends and their packhorses. But they were not immune to the chaos as the two mustang packhorses joined the fracas, trying to rid themselves of the burdens that kept them from escaping what they probably saw as certain death by the huge bear.

While Ezra and Otter fought the mustangs, Dove was trying to steady her buckskin and struggled with the reins of the gelding just as Otter's blue roan shouldered into the buckskin, startling the horse even more. Shouts, screams, whinnies, grunts, and more rattled the timber and two horses were splashing in the water at the edge of the small pond. And if that wasn't enough, nature itself joined the melee with a rattling aftershock to the earthquake. The trees were swaying, boulders from high above loosened and pushed rockslides before them as they tumbled into the trees that fought to hold tight to the soil in their roots, but some gave way and lay down before the slides.

Gabe shouted, "Go back! Go back!" and swung Ebony around, jerking the little sorrel behind him. He reached down and caught the rein of Otter's blue roan just behind the headstall and pulled him around beside his black. He reached back and smacked the gelding on the rump and slapped legs to the big stallion to follow. Dove crowded before Otter, Wolf was on the heels of the roan and Ezra had already turned his bay and the mustang behind him and he led the way at a run down the narrow trail to creek bottom.

When they rode into the flat at the bottom, Ezra reined up, looking around for Dove and the others, relieved when he saw each one come alongside. They all turned to look at the trail and saw the men of the Agaidika band come out of the timber, frantically gigging their horses through the trees. Within moments, almost everyone made it clear and when looking back at the narrow canyon, saw the rising cloud of dust from the crashing of the rockslide that buried the pool of water and dammed the stream. Gabe looked at Ezra, "Did they all make it?"

Ezra looked at the gathered warriors, obviously counting, then turned back to Gabe,

"Looks like a couple missing." It would be days before the water found its way out and into the stream where the band now waited, but the natural force of water would find a way.

Gabe saw several warriors animatedly speaking with their chief and gesturing his way. He frowned and leaned toward Otter, "What's that all about? They act like it's our fault." Before she could answer, Owitze and Shoots Running Buffalo rode close and the chief asked, "Is it true that you said this would happen?"

Gabe frowned, looked at Otter, and the woman answered for him. "Yes, I told Shoots Running Buffalo that my man, Spirit Bear, said there would be another time of the mountains shaking, and that it would not be as bad as the last."

The chief looked at Gabe, "How do you know this?"

Gabe dropped his eyes, breathed deep, and looked at the chief, "I have been through earthquakes before and there always follows one or two or more times where smaller quakes happen. Those that know about these call them aftershocks, or shocks that come after the big one."

"So, this always happens?" asked the chief.

"Yes."

"How many?"

"That I don't know. Sometimes just one time, others . . ." he shrugged, unknowing.

"We lost two men and their horses, if we had known, perhaps that would not happen." The chief frowned as he looked at Gabe, expecting a response.

"If I had known when it would happen, I would've told you. I just knew it would happen, but I could not know when," answered Gabe.

The chief grunted, nodded, and turned away. With a wave of his hand, he started the column toward the trail that cut through the black timber on the face of the mountain.

The shadows of the towering mountains stretched across the valley bottom, blending with the black timber that now covered the mountain sides as well as the canyon bottom. The trail began to climb away from the creek, snaking through the timber and showing years of use with well-traveled and cleared paths. Where game trails would often have branches hanging low across the trail, the shadowing trees had been cleared by the passage of many large animals, including horse-mounted travelers.

The band of warriors had stretched out single file and Gabe and company followed suit. Wolf scampered in and out of the trees, always searching, sniffing, hunting for small game, but finding none, always returned to the side of Otter aboard her blue roan that had become friends with the big wolf. The route was now a steady climb and switched back on itself time and again as they rose toward the crest of the flat-topped mountain. The forest changed from towering ponderosa to skinny and thick growing lodgepole and soon showed spruce and fir. As they neared the crest they passed scattered juniper, some white bark pine and an occasional bristlecone. They were glad to be out of the canyon bottom, thinking it would be safer away from the possible rockslides and more and hoping to find a safe campsite for a restful night.

5 / Mountaintop

When they crested the mountain after the long switch-back trail climbed through the black timber, they reined up and stepped down to give the horses a blow. Gabe leaned back, arching his back bone and stretching his long legs, breathing deep of the clear mountain air. He stepped to the side and took a long gander at the surrounding country. It was as if they stood on top of the world and God had smoothed out the mountaintops and patted them down with the palm of his hand. For several miles in all directions, the flat-topped mountains stretched before them, showing little but the short grasses and tundra of the alpines, occasional patches of blue and purple columbine waved in the cold air to add a touch of color to the panorama. Far beyond the scarred and marred flat-tops rose granite peaks, holding patches of snow and glaciers beckoning the weary travelers onward like lonely widows waving silken hankies from forlorn windows.

The Indians started walking to the right toward a long dip that held greener grass and the promise of water. Sitting Turtle drew close to Gabe and said, "We will camp there," pointing with his chin, "no wind, and there is water."

Gabe looked to the west where the distant mountains cradled the sun as it shot its golden lances across the sky, turned to the others, "Looks like we'll be beddin' down yonder. Turtle says its outta the wind and that suits me."

Otter glanced at the swale that offered the campsite, then offered the reins of the blue roan to Gabe, "There is no firewood there. You take the horses, Dove and I will get firewood, there," pointing to the backtrail where it crested the hilltop. Several scraggly white bark pine marked the trail and offered slim pickings for firewood, but the swale with the grass and water held none. Gabe nodded, took the roan and started after the others, followed closely by Ezra, leading the buckskin and the grulla mustang. Wolf trotted after the women.

The women spotted a long dead and twisted snag of white bark pine with skeletal branches reaching for the darkening sky. A log of a sister tree lay at its base and the women began gathering armloads of the dry branches. Wolf bellied down, watching the women pick up the branches and stack them to the side, his tongue lolled out the side of his mouth and his eyes showed interest as he watched. He quickly came to his feet, staring down the slope into the thick timber. His head lowered and a low growl came from deep within. Otter noticed when he came to his feet and now watched the wolf. She snapped her fingers at Dove and both women looked at the wolf then down toward the trees where he watched. Wolf took a tentative step forward, lips curling over his teeth, as he began to growl.

"Go get the men!" ordered Otter to Dove, as she drew near the wolf. Dove took off at a run, never looking back and trying for all she was worth to get to the men without shouting. Ezra happened to look as he pulled at the lead lines of the grulla mustang and saw Dove coming at a run. He spoke to Gabe over his shoulder, "Somethin's wrong!"

Gabe turned, saw Dove running toward them, then quickly swung aboard the black, dropping the reins and lead line of the packhorses, and slapped legs to Ebony. The big horse lunged forward, digging his hooves into the tundra, and was at a run instantly. Within seconds, Gabe was approaching Otter, who was on her knees beside Wolf, holding on to the black beast with fingers dug into his scruff. Gabe brought Ebony to a sliding stop and was on the ground before the stallion stopped. His rifle in hand, he ran to the side of his woman and looked down the slope. Coming toward them was snarling, snapping silver-tip boar grizzly charging up the steep hill, hampered only by the logs and limbs on long dead trees that cluttered the mountainside. He paddled over each log as if it were nothing more than a twig, roaring his contempt with every lunge.

Gabe dropped to one knee, eared back the hammer on the Ferguson and took a quick aim. He caught the front blade between the buckhorn sight at the rear, centered it on the chin of the charging bear and squeezed off the shot. Smoke belched from the pan, more from the muzzle as the big bore rifle bucked and spit led. Before the smoke cleared, Gabe had dropped the rifle, spun the trigger guard to open the breech, and fed ball, patch, powder into the breech, and powder into the pan. He snapped the pan down, spun the trigger guard to close the breech and brought the rifle to his shoulder. His years of practice had sped the process and no more than five seconds had passed when the stock nestled against his shoulder. A quick sight, easily done as the bear was no more than fifteen feet away, and another blast echoed between the mountains in chorus with the bellowing roar of the charging grizzly.

Gabe snatched the pistol from his belt, cocking the hammer as he brought it up and with only a glimpse of brown through the smoke, let loose the messenger of death to greet the massive bruin. The bullet from the Bailes over/under pistol entered the growling mouth of the beast and bored into its brain, splattering blood and bone over the hump on its back. The mammoth of the mountains slid to a stop, his teeth touching the moccasin of Gabe who was frantically twisting the revolving barrels of the pistol and cocking the second hammer for another shot, but the bear's dying breath exhaled it stink and blood on the moccasins and leggings of its killer.

Wolf had not left the side of Otter, but she loosed the beast just as the bear neared and as the bear slid to a stop, Wolf lunged at its throat and sunk his teeth into the thick fur but the bear was dead and Wolf stepped back, brown fur dangling from his teeth as he looked from Gabe to Otter. The woman had wrapped her arms around Gabe from behind and buried her face in his neck. Words were unnecessary, as Gabe clasped his woman's arms, and leaned back into her embrace. He was breathing deeply, not realizing he had held his breath throughout the attack. He shook his head, then spoke softly to Otter, "Don't you ever go anywhere in these mountains without a weapon!"

Otter giggled, "That's what I have you for!"

Ezra and Dove came beside them, started to say something but were interrupted, "Aiiieee! He killed a grizzly!" shouted Shoots Running Buffalo. Others cried out with shouts and war cries, all echoing across the canyon below. They gathered around, looking at the huge bear, chattering about the beast and the man known as Spirit Bear. Several went to Gabe, slapping him on the back, exclaiming about the bear and what a great warrior he was, and more.

Otter stood, offered her hand to Gabe and he stood beside her, and as he stood he realized how weak he felt, knowing it was the fear and more that made him stumble, but caught himself with the arm of Otter. He grinned at Ezra as his friend said, "Good shootin' my friend."

"I coulda used some help," mumbled Gabe, forcing a grin.

"Why? There was only one!" answered Ezra, somberly, then letting a slow grin paint his face.

Ebony stood several feet away, reins trailing on the ground, but his wide eyes showed he was not comfortable being this close to a grizzly and Gabe went to him, picked up the reins and stroked his neck, speaking softly to the big stallion. Most horses would have jumped and run at the first smell of the grizzly, but Ebony and Gabe had a bond of trust that neither would break, and the horse had done as bidden, fought his natural fear and tendency to run, and stayed where he was left, waiting for his friend.

Owitze came to the side of Gabe, put his hand on his shoulder and said, "This was the bear we saw at the pool before the rockslide. There is grey dust in his fur."

"I wondered about that. Didn't expect to see another boar this close. He was an old one."

"We will help you with the bear," offered the chief.

Gabe nodded, then asked, "I've never eaten bear, is it good?"

Owitze grinned, "This is *daza-meà,* the moon of summer starting. The bears eat greens and berries; their meat is good. But in the time of colors or *ye-ba-meà,* when they eat rotting flesh, and fish, they are not so good."

Gabe turned to Otter, grinned, "Then if you and Dove will start the rest of supper, we'll skin out ol' grizz and bring you some fresh steaks!"

Otter smiled, motioned to Dove, and the women corralled one of the younger warriors to help carry the wood, and they started back to the campsite. Otter looked at the young man with his arms full and said, "You will take some pack horses back to the others for the bear." The young man grinned and nodded, glad that he would have a responsibility other than helping the women.

6 / Village

Otter and Dove fashioned a travois from the lodge-pole pine that covered the eastern slope of the mesa. They had passed through the thin limbed trees as they traversed the face of the mountain on the switchback trail. It had been a task to get the grulla mustang pack-horse to trail the travois laden with the hide and meat of the grizzly, none of the horses liked the smell of the beast who was their natural predator and all were skittish when first brought near the packed travois, but eventually the men were successful and were now on their way to the village. Ezra led the grulla at the end of the line, keeping the cargo as far away from the other horses as possible.

They had an early start and the trail bore southwest across the adjoining flat top mesas. By mid-day they dropped off the mesa by way of a switchback trail that descended the steep and rocky slope into the lake strewn valley below that had the riders bending back over the cantles of their saddles, balancing the horses as they stepped and slid down the precipitous path. When Owitze signaled a stop, Otter shook her head as Gabe grumbled, "'bout time. I was almost ready to pull off and stop by our own selves and let them go on."

"I believe the village is near," replied a somber Otter.

Gabe noticed her expression and frowned, "Is there something wrong?"

Otter forced a smile, shaking her head, "No, it is a hard trail and I am tired."

Gabe nodded, thinking there was more to her mood than she admitted but chose to let it be as they dismounted and loosened the girths on the saddles to give the horses a breather. It was to be a brief stop and he dug in the parfleche for some smoked meat and passed it around to Ezra, Dove and Otter, who declined the offer.

She walked to a large boulder and sat down to lean against the stone, pushing her hair back and stretching out. She looked across the rocky flats, felt the cool breeze on her face and idly picked up a twig and tossed it aside. Dove went to her side and sat down, saying nothing, just being with her sister. It was not often the two spent time together and the men chose to walk away and give them time alone.

***

Dove knew the moods of her sister and she sat silently beside her, waiting for her to speak if she chose to, but by her presence, letting her sister know she was there for her. The cool breeze came from the pockets of snow still cradled in the high mountain crags that clawed at the clear blue of the morning sky, and Otter leaned back against Dove's shoulder as the sisters shared their warmth. "The village of Owitze is the village of Moon Walker," said Otter, quietly.

Dove looked at her sister, eyes wide, and asked, "From the encampment?" She spoke of the grand encampment that occurred about every three summers when many bands from the different branches of the Shoshone gathered for the spring dance and to prepare for the summer hunts. The grand encampment was the spring of the previous year and before Gabe and Ezra came into the camp of the Shoshone. It was a time when courtships between bands happen and many take their life mates. Moon Walker was a young warrior from the Bannock that allied with the *Agaieka* Shoshone of the north and had often sought out Pale Otter to pursue her in the typical courtship ritual. But Otter's father thought she was too young, and Moon Walker was not a suitable mate for her and he would not accept an arrangement for marriage.

Dove sat quietly for a moment, then said, "Maybe he is no longer with this band. He is not among these."

"The young warrior, Running Badger, that carried

the wood for us is his brother, but he did not know me."

"Are you not happy now? With Spirit Bear as your mate?" asked Dove, hesitantly.

Otter paused, and the quiet moment spoke loudly, then answered, "I am proud of Spirit Bear and I have been happy with him. But I did not believe I would ever see Moon Walker again." She reached down to run her fingers through the scruff of Wolf's neck, drawing him closer to her as she sighed heavily. "Maybe he has taken a mate of his own and has left this band."

Dove looked at her sister, knowing not what to say, but feeling her turmoil of emotions. When she had been with Moon Walker, the sisters had spent several nights staying awake and talking about the courtship ritual and what Otter hoped to have with Moon Walker. But when the Bannock band left, the dreams they shared had been shattered and the sisters wept together. But late that same summer, Gabe and Ezra came into their camp and by the moon of *naa-meá,* Moon Walker had been forgotten and the sisters were pledged to the men who would become their mates. As she thought of her sister, she hoped they would not see Moon Walker and their lives would not be changed.

***

As the band of hunters rode into the camp, women and children ran to their men, greeting them happily but cheerful faces soon grew long when the news of the lost buffalo herd spread. When the villagers saw the visitors, they drew back, especially when they saw the black wolf that walked beside the woman on the blue roan horse. Others stared at the man with Dove, as most had never seen a man of color that had hair like a buffalo, and they gawked and drew back, suspicious of these strangers that rode with Shoshone women.

Owitze came to Gabe, "There is a lodge, there," he pointed to a tipi at the edge of the village, "that you and your people may use while you are with us. We will have a feast later where you will meet the other leaders of our village."

"Chief, we are honored and grateful. We have some bison and of course the bear meat that we would like to give to your people for the feast tonight," replied Gabe.

The chief looked at the white man, frowned, "You do not need to do this."

"But we would be honored if you would accept it. You have been gracious to take us into your village and give us the use of a lodge, it is only right we share with your people."

The chief nodded, motioned to two of his warriors and with Gabe's direction, the men took the meat away for the women of the village to prepare.

The village had about sixty lodges that sat on the uphill side of a beautiful placid lake that lay like a mirror reflecting the image of the rimrock butte on the far shore. The pristine lake showed deep waters of indigo blue across most of its one-mile length. The opposite shore was about five hundred yards away and lay at the base of the sloping grassy shoulder of the tall butte. The village lay on the east bank and was nestled between the water and the thick ponderosa, spruce and fir that made up the black timber around the three sides of the lake opposite the rimrock butte. It was a beautiful and serene setting and once the curiosity passed, the people were welcoming.

Gabe and Ezra stripped the gear from the horses as Dove and Otter arranged the parfleches and packs. Once the horses were unencumbered, the men led them to the edge of the camp where the herd of the villagers was grazing and let their horses run. When they returned to the lodge, the women had already staked out the grizzly hide and begun scraping the membrane, readying the hide for tanning. It would be an involved process, but one that would yield a warm covering for winter cold. As Gabe looked at the hide, he guessed it to be at least ten feet, maybe as much as twelve feet from tail to nose and the same from tip to tip of front paws. He knelt down to look more closely at the paws and placed his two hands side by side and saw there was still paw showing on either side of his hands. He shook his head at the massive size of the beast and looked at the women, "He's a big 'un!"

Otter nodded, "The two bullets from your rifle hit

here," she pointed to two holes about a handbreadth apart on what was the chest of the bear, "and your pistol bullet ruined his head. I will have to have brains from another to tan the hide." She nodded to the big hole at the top of the hide where the skin had been peeled back from the skull, or what remained of it. "There were also old wounds," she pointed to one on either side of the hide that would have been in the chest and belly of the beast where healed scars were evident. "Maybe from arrows or another bullet from someone."

"If that's all they got into him, he probably ate them for dinner!" declared Ezra, looking at the huge hide.

"His fur is still good. If it had been later, he would have shed much of it and it would only be good for the leather. But he had a thick fur, so . . ." she dropped to her knees and stretched out to continue scraping.

***

It was a bountiful feast, made so by the addition of the bear and bison meat. With the bear meat being a rarity, it soon disappeared, but with bison, elk, deer, and mountain sheep meat as well as several trout, there was ample meat for everyone. And the women did an exceptional job of adding a good variety of mountain berries, roots, bulbs, and shoots to round out the sumptuous feast.

Gabe and Ezra sat with the leaders of the village

while Dove and Otter shared duties with the women. *Owitze,* Twisted Hand, was joined by *Weahwewa*, Wolf Dog, at the prominent place of the feast and Gabe learned that the men were joint chiefs of the bands that made up the village. Shoots Running Buffalo sat beside Gabe and spoke with him throughout the meal. On the far side of Ezra, another warrior and war leader, Moon Walker, sat and shared in the conversation.

"In two days, our bands will separate, go on the summer hunts. It is tradition that the groups are smaller, often members of the same families. We come together in the time of colors to stay together through the cold moons," explained Shoots, between bites.

"So, your hunting party that we met was not a part of that?" asked Gabe.

"No, we were scouting for buffalo and if we could, we would take some before returning. But the great shaking of the earth did not allow that."

Moon Walker leaned forward, "What shaking?"

Shoots Running Buffalo looked at the other war leader and began explaining about the earthquake, how the mountains shook, and trees fell and rocks tumbled. "The buffalo, a great herd, ran from the mountains. We were afraid and rode from the canyon quickly, but the horses were scared, and they were hard to handle."

"We have felt the earth move before," declared Moon Walker.

"Aiieee, not like this! The very mountains shook like the leaves on the quakies!" declared Shoots. He looked at Ezra, "That man told his people before it happened, and they left their camp, or they would have been trampled by the buffalo. And this one," pointing with his chin to Gabe, "Told us it would happen again, and it did!"

Moon Walker sat his wooden platter down, wiped his fingers on his buckskin leggings as he looked at the two men, "Are you *boha grande?*"

"No, we are not shaman. But there are things we know and can see," explained Ezra, continuing to eat.

Moon Walker looked at Gabe, "Pale Otter is your woman?"

Gabe frowned, sat his trough down, and looked at the man as he wiped off his hands. "Yes. We were joined last fall, in the month of *ezhe'i-mea'* before the snows came."

Moon Walker looked at Ezra, "And you have taken her sister, Grey Dove?"

Ezra scowled at the man, "Grey Dove is my wife, yes."

Moon Walker slowly nodded his head, stood and left the circle, disappearing into the darkness.

7 / Separation

Gabe looked at Shoots Buffalo Running and asked, "What was that about?"

Shoots dropped his gaze to the fire in the circle then looked back at Gabe and Ezra, "Moon Walker is Bannock, but his mother is Agaideka Shoshone. When his father took her to wife, it was not as common as it is now, and she was not accepted into the band. After their son came, it was better, but his mother, Rabbit Tail, was a hard woman. Her hatred poisoned him, and he is against any woman that joins herself to anyone from a different tribe."

"Well, he sure acted like he had a burr under his blanket, that's for certain. Will he try to do anything about it?" asked Gabe, glancing to Ezra who leaned forward to hear the conversation.

"I do not know. He has not before, but there is more," said Shoots, pausing and looking at the men. "At the

Grand Encampment, Moon Walker had asked Red Pipe for Pale Otter, but was refused. He believed it was because he was Bannock and was angry, and now you have come into our village with her as your woman, and he," nodding to Ezra, "has her sister as his woman."

Gabe glanced at Ezra then back to Shoots, "Is there anything he can do? I mean to make trouble or . . ." asked Gabe, shrugging as he looked at Shoots.

"Our customs allow a man to have more than one wife, but it is not allowed for a woman to have more than one husband, but if a woman chooses another, she can leave the man, or put the man out of her lodge," explained Shoots, a slight grin tugging at the corner of his mouth. "But that does not happen often."

Beyond the central fire circle, several drums had been set up and began their rhythmic beat, bringing many of the villagers to the circle to begin dancing. The drummers also began a chanting sing and were joined by many of the dancers. As the men started their toe stubbing and head bobbing movements, keeping time with the drums, the singing rose, and many joined in the high-pitched chants. Gabe and Ezra watched, mesmerized by the movements and song, and Shoots said, "This is just a time of dancing for we will soon separate for the summer hunts. Early in the *buhisea'-mea,* or what you call green-up, our people hold a Buffalo Dance to give thanks for the buffalo and to ask for a good hunt."

Gabe looked at Shoots, "Like a prayer to *Tam Apo*?"

Shoots grinned, pleased that Gabe knew of their term for the Great Spirit, and nodded his head in agreement.

There was a change in the beat of the drums as Gabe turned back to the dancers. Several had stepped aside and made way as Pale Otter stepped into the circle, followed by Wolf who stayed close by her side. As she moved, Wolf would run around her, and jump beside her, then he moved in front of her and jumped up to put his forepaws on her shoulder, facing her with his mouth open and tongue lolling, and bounced on his hind legs as Otter moved towards him, appearing as if they were joined together. The Shoshone hold the wolf in great respect, as they picture their creator god as a wolf and many of their legendary tales tell of the Wolf and the coyote, the trickster. But for them to see the big black beast dancing with one their own was such as moment as to silence everyone but the drummers and they beat their cadence and chanted their tribal songs. Gabe was proud of his woman and watched her and the people about her as she enjoyed the time with people of her tribe. But movement at the edge of the firelight caught Gabe's attention and he looked to see Moon Walker glaring at Otter and with a quick glance toward Gabe, turn and disappear into the darkness.

As Otter and Wolf tired, others rejoined the circle and resumed dancing as Otter led Wolf away from the circle. She came to stand behind Gabe, then dropped to one knee, one hand on Wolf as she asked Gabe, "Are you ready to go to our lodge?"

Gabe looked at her, grinned, and asked, "I dunno. Is it safe after you and Wolf been dancin' together?"

Otter playfully slapped him on the shoulder and stood, waiting for him to stand and go with her to the lodge. As he did, he saw Dove and Ezra also stand and start toward the tipi. Gabe put his arm around Otter's waist, and they walked together away from the firelight and into the darkness, but a glance to the heavens showed a starlit night with the almost full globe of the moon slowly rising to take its place among the stars.

***

First light showed a flurry of activity in the village. Tipis were coming down; horses were led into the camp and were being rigged to pack or ride. Shoots came to the lodge of Gabe and company, "Our people are going on the summer hunt. We go to different lands, go as families and more. With less people, easy to hunt and get enough meat for all." He paused as he looked at Gabe, then continued, "If you," nodding toward Gabe and the others, "would like to come with our family, we will hunt together."

Gabe looked back at Ezra, saw his slight nod, and

turned back to Shoots, "We would be honored to join you and your family. Is there anything special we need to do?"

Shoots grinned, "Bring your lodge and all you have. We will not return here."

"But isn't this someone's lodge?" asked Gabe.

"The woman who had this lodge, died and it is now yours."

Gabe swallowed hard, nodded, and said, "We'll get ready!"

***

With twelve lodges in their group, theirs was one of the larger bands and started out to the west, dropping off the rocky flats that held the picturesque lake that had been the site of their spring camp. The band stretched out with horses with travois, dogs with packs and warriors and women horseback. But the caravan moved well, Shoots in the lead with his woman, Laughing Antelope, at his side. Gabe and company stayed in the rear, letting the families stay with one another and with many of the horses and people still reserved about Wolf, it was best for them to be a little separated from the others.

They kept the south fork of the Yellowstone River, what would one day be called the Clark's Fork, to the south and upon entering a long valley, turned to the north. When the band stopped for nooning, Shoots came along the line speaking to others and when he came to Gabe's group, he seated himself and explained, "We will travel about four days. This valley leads to a trail that crosses the mountains and into a long valley. The river my people call Stillwater leads to the land of the buffalo beyond the mountains. We will camp in the valley by the river."

As Shoots started to leave, Gabe walked with him and once away from the others, Gabe asked, "Is Moon Walker with this group?"

Shoots glanced at Gabe, grinned, then answered, "No, his family has gone to the west to the land of the big lake."

"Does he have a woman or wife?" asked Gabe.

"He had a woman, but she died trying to give birth. The child died also. He has always been angry, even when he was very young, and that made him more angry. He is a man that is a good warrior and has been made a war leader among the people. He fights with that anger."

Gabe looked at Shoots, understanding that the man was not just helping him to understand, but warning him about the man who had displayed his anger even before Gabe knew anything about him. Gabe stopped, looked at Shoots, "I am grateful." The man nodded and walked away as Gabe returned to his friends.

***

It was a good, though often trying, journey with Gabe and Ezra usually hunting in the early morning or late evening hours and sharing the bounty with the others. After a challenging trek through the narrowing canyon, crossing the river time and again to make their way through the thick timber and narrow defiles made difficult by granite mountains crowding close in, the end of the trail was seen and by the end of the fourth day, they made their camp on the north side of the river, just before it made a dogleg bend around a high rocky point before opening up to the flat plains beyond. Shielded from the plains and with towering mountains to the east and west, their camp was easily defendable and had ample graze and water close at hand. Although the mouth of the valley held a wide alluvial sand plain formed in eons past, the valley and flats beyond were well watered and green, offering fine hunting land both in the flats and the foothills of the higher mountains.

The women were already chattering about the patches of camas and timpsila they found, and with the river bending back on itself, the edges held cattails with fresh shoots and more. There were ample berry bushes nearby and others back in the canyon that would provide sweets and berries for the making of pemmican. It appeared to be a bountiful place and everyone's spirits were high as they hustled to make their camp. Tipi frames were raised, hide covers drawn up and within a short time, the village took on the appearance of having been there since early spring.

Otter had chosen the spot for their tipi and it now stood further upstream than the others, close to the edge of the juniper that came down the mountain slope above. A thin line of juniper marched beside the river, but the nearness of the water as it cascaded over a rocky shoal midstream, let them enjoy the chuckling of the white water as it came from the canyon above. They picketed their horses within reach of both graze and water, and after fetching several armloads of firewood, the four settled down to enjoy their new camp. The women had started the evening meal and the long shadows of the mountains behind them began to climb the west facing slopes across the river, slowly dimming the light of day and heralding the coming of the night.

8 / Hunt

Gabe sat contemplative and somewhat melancholy as he clasped his hands together, holding one knee as he leaned back and watched the coming day dim the lanterns of the night sky. One stubborn one refused to lessen its brightness even as the sky around it changed from deep velvety black to the dim grey of early morning. He had spent his usual time in prayer and had been thinking about his sister Gwyneth, wondering how she was faring in Washington as the social maven she aspired to be with her up and coming lawyer husband. He chuckled to himself as he remembered their last night together at the social gathering of the season that had ended in the challenge to a duel. *I don't miss that nonsense, that's for sure. Why would I? With this,* waving his hand before him, *around me. I never imagined such beauty and magnificence, mountains that literally scratch the sky and vistas that defy description.* He lifted his eyes to the sky and remembered God's word in the book of Isaiah 40:26, *"Lift up your eyes on high, and behold who hath created these things."*

Gabe smiled at the remembrance and leaned back against the big rock to watch the morning light bend over the eastern mountains and slowly paint the east faces of the mountains behind him. As the light of day lifted the curtain of darkness he slipped the brass telescope from its case and lifted it to his eye. It was his nature to always know where he was and as much about the country around him as possible. He believed that it was only a man's knowledge of his surroundings that gave him the ability to overcome any obstacle placed in his way. Laziness, ignorance, and complacency, had caused the downfall of many, but Gabe believed it necessary to know his surroundings and that knowledge would give him an advantage and escape from those who would do him or his friends harm.

The Stillwater canyon opened to the plains, but the flatlands that lay to the north were scarred by deep ravines, gullies, and hillocks that could hide any number of animals or enemies. Yet the mouth of the canyon was wide and flat, offering little cover to anyone that would approach from the north. And the steep mountains of the Beartooth range on the east and west of the camp were too formidable to assault and the deep canyon of the Stillwater would make any attacker vulnerable as they would have to approach in a single file and the steep walled canyon would prevent any broad based attack. Gabe chuckled as he thought of Shoots Running Buffalo, the man with a long name but considerable wisdom, who had chosen their camp well.

He turned back to scan the steep faces of the mountains that sided the Stillwater. Mountains that rose almost a mile high above the valley floor and whose peaks rose above timberline, leaving the summits bare as the morning sun silhouetted them against the cloudless sky. Behind the finger ridge that stood over the camp and where Gabe now sat, was a long ravine that came from the edge of the timber high above. But less than a hundred yards from where he sat, a bald face slide area showed yellow, and Gabe grinned as he scanned the breakaway slide, recognizing the yellow as sulfur, the needed ingredient for his making of gunpowder. The cavern that held their cabin on the Popo Agie where they spent the previous winter had yielded a rich deposit of Saltpeter or Potassium Nitrate and he had packed a good amount of the refined material, hoping to find the needed sulfur. Now they could make their own gunpowder. He stood and started for the exposed face of the yellow mineral, it was a short climb away and he wanted to be certain it was sulfur, so he needed to gather at least a pouch full.

When Gabe walked back into camp, Otter looked

up from the cookfire, smiled and said, "I have a surprise for you!" and turned back to her cooking. Gabe walked over to where Ezra sat on a rock and brought out the pouch, opened it and reached in to bring out a handful of the yellow mineral. Ezra looked, reached out to feel and smell the powdery yellow substance, then looked at Gabe, grinning, "Sulfur!"

"Ummhmm, now we can make our own gunpowder," suggested Gabe.

"Did you bring the saltpeter?" asked Ezra, frowning.

Gabe grinned, "Of course I did. We can get started mixing after breakfast. It'll probably take us a few tries to get it right, but I'm confident we can do it."

"Then we need to find some Galena or copper, something to make the bullets," added Ezra.

"That's a lot easier to find than sulfur, but there's a whole mountainside of sulfur up there," he pointed back to the long ridge that stood over the camp and the mountain behind it.

"What else did you see from up there?" asked Ezra, knowing the habit of his friend of scoping their surroundings.

"A lot of beautiful country. This valley opens up to some rough dry land with a lot of hills, mesas, and ravines, but some good flat land that might have some buffalo. And all around us on both sides and back thataway," nodding to the upstream of the Stillwater, "a lot of mountains. I caught a glimpse of some Bighorns over there," pointing to the far side of the river and the black timbered mountains, "looks like one o' these mountain streams comes from a high-country valley, but it looks like we'd hafta go on foot. Too steep to take the horses and I didn't see sign of any trails, but we can have a closer look."

Dove had heard the mention of Bighorn Sheep and came close, "The sheepskin makes soft leather and the big horns can be used for many things."

Ezra grinned, "Are you saying you want me to get you some Bighorns?"

Dove smiled, nodded, running her hands down her hips, "Very soft leather," and giggled.

Ezra looked at Dove, glanced at Gabe, and said, "What's a fella to do?"

Gabe chuckled, "Go hunting, I guess."

Otter's surprise was a pair of duck eggs, fried in the fat of the grizzly bear, and served up with strips of smoked bison. Gabe grinned every moment as he savored the rare delicacy and drew Otter beside him on the flat rock as they ate. She had gathered enough for everyone and they all enjoyed the rarity, leaving only tidbits of meat for Wolf, but Otter added a handful of trimmings dipped in the grease to satisfy the beast.

***

The sun had yet to crest the eastern mountains when

Gabe and Ezra mounted up and started upstream for their hunt. The cut that marked the spot where Gabe had viewed the Bighorns was just over a mile from their camp, but they crossed the river, and mounted a bald rise that held a stream that met the Stillwater with fresh snowmelt from the high country. After picketing the horses in the shade of the trees, the men were ready to assault the mountain. Gabe replaced his belt pistol with one of the saddle pistols, explaining, "Since I'm taking my bow, I thought one of these would be a little more firepower. I mean, after all, this'ns .62 caliber and that'ns only .54."

Ezra shook his head, "Do you really think anything you shoot with that thing is gonna know the difference in the size of the bullet?"

Gabe chuckled, "S'pose not, but I will. After that little nose to nose meeting with that grizz, I'm a little more cautious."

"Then why don't you take your rifle?"

"You're takin' yours, aren't you? 'Sides, it's easier to climb mountains carryin' this," nodding to his Mongol bow, "than that!" pointing to the Ferguson still in the scabbard. "And if we have to pack out a sheep or two . . ." he offered, letting Ezra draw his own conclusions.

***

They moved as stealthy and quiet as the most skilled woodsmen, but even if they made noise, it wouldn't be heard. Beside them chattered a white-water stream that cascaded over the rocks of the creek bed, rushing its way to the valley floor. They moved through the big ponderosa and spruce, watching every opening for any sign of movement or patch of fur that would be a giveaway. Within a short distance, they broke from the trees into a small clearing that afforded them a view of the stream and the limestone cliffs that shouldered the narrow ravine. They heard it before they saw it, but when they rounded a slight point, the crashing of whitewater as it cascaded from high above, dropping over a hundred feet to a small pool and huge boulders below, showed like a white ribbon against the black rock and timber. The waterfall was mesmerizing, and the men stopped and stared, looking at the magnificent sight that defied description while eliciting awe from the hardened men of the wilderness.

Gabe had, as was his custom, already nocked an arrow and now held the bow at his side as he took in the view, but other movement at the corner of his eye caught his attention. He moved only his eyes and saw the dingy white rump of a bighorn standing on a narrow ledge at the face of the cliff across the small stream. The ram was looking at them, and Gabe did not move except to use his elbow to touch Ezra and speak softly, "Don't move, ram, cliff." The confident bighorn turned his head away to look at his footing, and Gabe brought up the bow and loosed the arrow. But his rushed shot missed and the arrow clattered against the cliff, startling the ram who with one leap, started to scamper across the face of the rugged cliff, until the rifle in the hand of Ezra barked and the bullet took the ram, making him stumble and fall to the water below.

When the bighorn splashed in the water, Ezra dropped his rifle and sprung past Gabe, watching the body of the ram tumble over the rocks. Ezra quickly waded into the water, determined to retrieve his prize as it washed toward him, bouncing off the rocks, and tumbling with the cascading white-water. When it neared, Ezra, now hip deep in the water, grabbed the full curl horns and leaned back to drag the sheep with him to the shore. Gabe reached out and pulled Ezra with a hand on his collar and the other under an arm, pulling him to the shore. Ezra fell forward, his fall pulling the ram with him, and the bank held as the two men struggled together to retrieve the carcass.

"Whoooeeeee! That water is like ice! I'm numb from my waist down!" declared Ezra, stumbling onto the grassy bank. It was a narrow strip of grass, but mostly moss-covered rock, that offered solid footing. Ezra immediately started gathering broken branches, sticks and more to start a warming fire. Gabe went to where he dropped his gear and possibles pouch and retrieved the makings for starting a fire and the men soon had a fire going to try to dry off and warm up. As they knelt before the small fire, rubbing their hands together and slapping their legs, they looked at the ram and Ezra said, "She better be happy!" thinking of Dove and her implied request for the 'soft leather' of the sheep.

They made short work of dressing out the ram and while Gabe carried Ezra's rifle, he carried the ram. It was just a short distance to the horses, and they were ready to start back to camp, Gabe in the lead. But when they approached the tree line, he reined up and stood in his stirrups. He motioned for Ezra to come alongside and pointed toward the twisting Stillwater. At the edge of a wide bend of the river, a big bull moose was wading knee deep, dropping his head into the water and coming up with greenery hanging from his mouth as he feasted on the tidbits from the bottom. "What do you think? Should we take him?" asked Gabe.

Ezra watched the big moose, looked at his friend, "Nah, let's save him for another day. 'Sides, he looks too old and tough."

Gabe chuckled, put his heels to Ebony and moved into the clearing. The big moose looked over his shoulder at the two mounted men, but, unconcerned, dropped his head into the water for another mouthful of greens. The men chuckled, shaking their heads, and pointed the horses downstream toward camp.

9 / Scout

After their early morning hunt for the bighorn, Gabe and Ezra spent much of the afternoon formulating their collected minerals. With the powdery deposit of potash or saltpeter from the cave by the Popo Agie river, the sulfur from Gabe's recent find on the mountain, and the charcoal, they applied the formula of six parts saltpeter, one-part charcoal, and one-part sulfur. After grinding each mineral into a fine powder, they mixed the three into a small batch and tested it with a spark from the flint and steel used to start the fires. The resultant puff of an explosion told them they were on the right track and they loaded a pistol with their new mixture, which performed perfectly.

"By jove, I think you've got it!" declared Ezra, rocking back on his heels after watching Gabe cautiously fire the pistol. They had used a finer grind for the flash pan, and both the pan and the shot did just as expected.

"Well, that solves one problem, but we still need to find some galena or copper, but that'll come in time," resolved Gabe.

"*Behne!*" the greeting brought Gabe and Ezra around to see Shoots and Sitting Turtle coming towards them. Gabe lifted his hand and returned the greeting, then sat on the flat boulder Ezra had chosen for a seat.

"What are you shooting?" asked Turtle, grinning at the men.

"Oh, just clearing out my pistol," answered Gabe, lifting the Bailes turnover pistol for the two to see.

Both nodded as they came near and Shoots began, "Your women work on the horns and hide of a big-horn," nodding back toward Dove who was scraping the hide.

Gabe nodded toward Ezra, "That's his doin'. We went up on the mountain yonder, where that water-fall splits the timber. Dove wanted one for the soft leather," chuckled Gabe, elbowing Ezra as he spoke.

Both Shoots and Turtle grinned, knowing the way of the women and the soft leather of the mountain sheep. They sat on another of the flat rocks, "Our men will be on the scout for buffalo tomorrow." He pointed to the mouth of the canyon, "The herds gather in the flats there, but the hills and gullies can hide them. We are in Crow lands, but this is where Shoshone, Bannock, Blackfoot, and Crow hunt the buffalo. We cannot stay long in the open where the herds stay, we must scout them, plan a one-day hunt, and return to our camp. Most tribes do not fight when they hunt, unless . . ." he shrugged as he left the thought hang between them. Both knew there was nothing certain between tribes that often raided in each other's territory.

"Will all the men go on this scout?" asked Gabe, uncertain if this was an invitation or a caution.

"Most will. We separate in small groups to scout more of the flats and places where the herds may be; the more scouts the sooner we find the buffalo."

"Should we go with you?" asked Ezra, looking at Shoots.

"It would be good to have two more scouts," answered Shoots.

Gabe grinned, "We'll be ready. First light?"

Shoots nodded and stood to leave. He turned back to Gabe, "It would be good if there is no shooting. If there are others scouting and hear, they would find our camp."

Gabe slowly lifted his head in a nod, understanding what the war leader was saying, and said, "No more."

Shoots grinned, and the two men walked away. Gabe turned to Ezra, "I was too focused on getting the formula down for the powder, I didn't even think about the possibility of other tribes scouting the area. I think we'd be alright with the Crow, but Blackfoot, I dunno."

Ezra dropped his gaze, stood and walked a few paces away and turned back to face Gabe. "What are we doing?"

Gabe frowned, looked at Ezra and answered, "We're mixing gunpowder, what'd you think?"

"No, I mean what are *we* doing? We didn't come out here to fight Indians, hunt buffalo, and wander around on the flat lands. It seems all we've done the last two summers was to get ready to hole up for the winter. Hunt an' hide, hunt an' hide. What happened to our dreams of discoverin' and explorin'?" Ezra shook his head, picked up a stone and chucked it at the river, trying to skip it off the smooth water of the eddy. He looked back at a confounded Gabe and waited for him to answer.

Gabe dropped his eyes to the burn mark on the stone where they fired the sample powder the looked at Ezra. His shoulders sagged as he stood and walked to his friend, picked up a stone and mimicked Ezra's attempt at skipping the flat rock across the whirlpool, but he failed as did Ezra.

"I reckon its kinda like that whirlpool. It's goin' one way and the rest of the river's goin' t'other. Seems like everything we come up against is set against us. The Blackfoot, the Crow, the earthquake, the buffalo, all goin' one way and we're wantin' to go t'other. I guess I fell into the trap of circumstance and got comfortable travelin' with the Shoshone and Bannock, prob'ly cuz it was safer. But you're right, it's not what we dreamed of or planned on doin'." He stretched, looked around, "We've seen some mighty pretty country. Those mountains," nodding his head to the Beartooth range behind them, "seem to keep a lot of secrets. It's one thing to look at them, big as they are, lookin' like their holdin' the sky up like pillars on an ancient Greek Temple, holding patches of snow high up where we'll never go, and givin' a home to elk, moose, bighorns, mountain goats, deer, and who knows what all." He paused, folded his arms across his chest, then turned back to Ezra, "How 'bout we go on this buffalo hunt with Shoots and his people, get us some fresh meat smoked and maybe another buffalo robe, then we'll head on north like we intended. That country's just like this, never been charted and seldom seen by anybody but natives, true uncharted territory!"

Ezra grinned, "Now you're talkin'. This hunt and such won't take more'n a couple days, then we could be on our way!"

Gabe grinned in response, "Sounds 'bout right to me!"

***

One old man, Buffalo Hump, Sitting Turtle, and two young men, Black Badger and Red Bird, stayed in the camp with the women and children and watched the others leave for the buffalo scout. Ten warriors plus Gabe and Ezra rode together to the mouth of the canyon of Stillwater River. Another unnamed stream joined the Stillwater from the west and about two

miles further, another small stream from the south
east melded its water with the Stillwater. It was at this
confluence that Shoots stopped the hunting party and
divided the band into three groups. "You," growled
Shoots, motioning to a big chested man, "Standing
Bear. You take three men, take next stream west, find
herd, come back here." Shoots twisted around, spotted another, motioned him forward, "Four Horns,
take three at red dirt, go that way," pointing to the
northwest, "across flats, find buffalo, come back here."

Shoots motioned to Gabe and Ezra to come near,
"You will be with me and Wolf Dog."

Gabe nodded, and moved alongside Shoots as the
band continued downstream along the Stillwater.
Within a short distance, Standing Bear and his group
separated and about a mile and a half further, Four
Horns and his three men took to the low hills across
the red dirt flats.

The second group had no sooner dropped behind a
long ridge, than Shoots led the remainder up a slight
slope of no more than a couple hundred feet to a bald
ridge that bent with the river below. As soon as they
crested, he stopped, slid from his horse and motioned
the others to do the same. There in the wide grassy
flats north of the river, grazed a large herd of buffalo.
The valley was less than a mile wide, and the herd
stretched out at least a mile downstream, with many
having crossed the Stillwater to the greener grass on

the south side. Several thousand buffalo slowly milled about, grazing contentedly on the tall grass. Near the bluff, two young bulls clashed, kicking up dust as they bellowed and threatened, then charged at one another, butting heads and bouncing back. Others watched, but most were disinterested in the sparring practice of the youngsters. Further down the edge of the ridge that boxed in the valley, an old bull rolled in a dust pit, watched by a cow and her orange coated calf.

Closer to the hunters, a big bull walked, head swinging side to side, beard touching the ground, followed by two young bulls, probably the second generation of this old herd bull. Throughout the herd, mothers tended their youngsters, nursing and pushing them around, while juveniles ran and played, jumping and twisting as they kicked and cavorted. Gabe looked to the sun, guessed it to be about an hour past mid-day, and thought they had come about a dozen miles from their camp. The men sat or knelt beside their horses as they watched the herd and Gabe asked Shoots, "Do we take any now?"

"No. We will wait until the others are with us, at first light we bring all. The women need to be here to butcher and skin right away. When we hit the herd, they will move. We want to take all we need in first hunt." He paused, looking around, then added, "We are in Crow lands. Blackfoot, this many," holding up three, then four fingers, "days that way," pointing to the northwest. "We hunt, take in one day, leave herd to others."

Gabe realized the wisdom of Shoots decision. If they took any buffalo now, they had no packhorses or travois with them and the men would have to do all the work, leaving them vulnerable to attack by others. Even if they sent someone back for the women and packhorses, they could not get here until dusk at the earliest, probably well after dark. Then they would be exposed to attack on another day. But by returning to the village, getting an early start on the morrow, then the hunt and butchering could be done in one day, men always available to defend against attack, and they could be gone by dark.

Shoots scooted backwards, drawing his horse with him and leading the others over the edge of the flat-top ridge. They mounted up and walked their horses from the valley, returning to the rendezvous with the others so they could return to camp. The sun was off their right shoulder when they met Four Horns and his men, and it was laying an orange cast across the land when Standing Bear returned. All were glad to hear of the sighting of a large herd, and as they rode alongside the chuckling river that caught golden splashes and bounced them back, each man was bragging about the buffalo they would kill on the morrow. But tomorrow always holds surprises, all anticipated, but not all of them are pleasant.

10 / Taken

The men were in good spirits, dusk was settling on the land and they were nearing their camp. Thoughts of a successful buffalo hunt the next day had filled their minds and they often talked and joked about what the hunt would hold. They were less than five miles from their camp when they passed the confluence of the West Fork of the Stillwater and spotted fresh tracks. Shoots stopped, leaned down to look, others came close, also looking at the obvious sign of many riders, both coming and going. Shoots looked at Gabe, then to the others, lifted his arm in the air and screamed his war cry and slapped legs to his mount, taking off at a gallop toward camp. Gabe and Ezra were close behind, both realizing what the tracks meant. Unbidden images of a bloody attack filled their minds as they raced toward the camp.

The big ridge that protruded into the canyon and

blocked any view of the camp served only to heighten their concern, especially when they saw thin spirals of dark smoke rising beyond. They rode around the point, lying low on their horses' necks, but the view before them brought them to a sudden halt. Smoke lifted from the remains of many lodges, blackened lodge poles stood barren of covering, two dead horses lay near the river, and many bodies, some charred, all bloody, lay scattered about.

Gabe and Ezra had reined up, then picked their way through the debris, still aboard their horses, standing in their stirrups to look toward the upper end of the village where their lodge had been, but only a tripod of lodgepole, all blackened by fire, stood. A quick glance across the stream to the wide meadow showed all the horses were gone, the body of one young man lay sprawled in the grass by the water.

Gabe and Ezra slid from their mounts, ran to the smoking debris to look for bodies, but there were none. Remains of parfleche and packs and packsaddles were stacked together, all blackened and burned, but there was no sign of Otter and Dove. Gabe searched the ground for tracks, started a wide circle, motioned for Ezra to go below while he went above the remains, and they searched for any sign that would show the women had fled safely. Gabe found tracks of an unfamiliar horse, but they were older, probably made early in the day, probably by one of the men that stayed behind.

Those tracks followed the tracks made by Gabe and Ezra when they went on the bighorn hunt and they were not of the women's horses.

When Ezra came near, Gabe pointed out the tracks, "But those weren't made by the women," he declared.

"But whose are they?" asked Ezra. "The raiders came from below and went back that way. Who was this?"

"I dunno. Maybe one of the men from the village went on a hunt like we did." He walked around a bit then pointed, "Look here. This is where he came back." Another set of tracks, the same horse, showed approaching the camp from upstream.

Ezra looked at the sign, bent to examine it closely, then said, "I dunno. These might have been made earlier than those," nodding toward the first tracks. "But maybe they are the later ones. Hard to tell, the ground is moist here and dry up there. But I don't think these were made by the raiders." He stood, took a deep breath. "Let's go see what Shoots thinks."

***

The men were digging through the rubble, throwing things in anger, screaming war cries and shouting their anguish and sorrow. Wives, mothers, children had been taken, others killed and left where they lay by the raiders. Shoots found his father, Buffalo Hump, an elder of the band, and his mother, side by side, both with their heads bashed in by some war club. The bodies of two Blackfoot warriors had been drug to the side, both mutilated by angry warriors. The bodies of Sitting Turtle, Black Badger and Red Bird had been mutilated and scalped by the Blackfoot raiders.

Shoots saw Gabe and Ezra walking toward him and knew by their expressions their women were either gone or dead. He stood, looking at them as they approached, then asked, "Are your women gone?"

Gabe answered, "Yes. Yours?"

"My woman and my son are gone, but my father and mother lay there," he nodded behind him toward the bodies of his parents.

"How many were taken?" asked Ezra, the muscles in his jaws working as he tried to contain his anger.

He flashed both hands, all fingers, then one hand with two fingers. "And your women."

"How many raiders?" asked Gabe, knowing it would be difficult to estimate the number, he had seen the tracks they followed to the camp and saw the turned soil where they left with their captives.

"Maybe four hands."

"What's the plan?" asked Gabe, anger flashing in his eyes.

"We will bury the dead then gather what supplies we can find. We will not come back to this camp."

"How 'bout me'n Ezra get our stuff together and head out to scout?"

"Standing Bear has gone. You follow, we will come soon," answered Shoots, struggling to keep his emotions in check. He had lost more than most, his family taken, his parents killed, and one of the young men left behind, Black Badger, was his son. Gabe and Ezra turned away, ran to the remains of their lodge and began digging through the rubble in hopes of finding anything they could take with them.

The packsaddles, parfleches, and panniers had been stacked on one side of the tipi and were covered with the remains and ashes from the hide lodge. Gabe tossed aside the burnt covers, digging into the still warm rawhide parfleches. He brought out hands full of smoked meat, held it up to Ezra, "Guess that's not hurt, maybe smoked a little more, but . . ." then something else caught his eye as he reached deeper into the bag. His fingers closed on the object and he brought it into the light, holding it almost reverently in his hands. It was a necklace of grizzly claws, interspersed with hand carved round wooden beads, but the ones at the center were separated by the fangs from the big bear. He looked at it, looked at Ezra who nodded, "Yeah, she was making it as a surprise for you. She was mighty proud of you and thought you should wear that everywhere."

Gabe slipped it over his head, felt it as it lay on his chest, sucked in a deep breath as he gritted his teeth in anger and sorrow, then went about the business of gathering what supplies they could find. They made up a pack of the extra gunpowder, two bars of lead, some bundles of dried timpsila and camas, a pouch of dried and ground biscuitroot, and a bundle of material and dried herbs for medicine and bandages. A second bundle was mostly the smoked meat. They had salvaged blankets to make up bedrolls and stashed the grizzly and buffalo hides in the rocks. It had been but a few minutes since they left Shoots and they rode to the gathering group that was busy preparing the bodies for burial. Shoots stood, came to their side, and said, "Find Standing Bear, stay together, wait for us."

"We will stay on their trail as long as the horses hold out. It's a good moon tonight and if we can, we'll keep after them. We'll leave sign, stacked rocks on the trail with more," explained Gabe. Shoots nodded, extended his hand and the men clasped forearms, then Gabe dug his heels into Ebony's side and the men left at a ground eating canter.

They rode in silence, but when the horses were well lathered, Ezra said, "We've got to rest the horses! Sides, it's gettin' too dark to see the trail."

Gabe had been leaning down from his saddle, searching the ground, and even with little light, they could easily see the trail. The raiders and their captives rode thirty horses or more and left a trail a child could follow, but he looked at Ezra, then to the lathered chest and flanks of Ebony and the bay of Ezra's and understood his friend. He reined up, pointed to the nearby cluster of aspen and stepped down to lead the horses to the little creek they followed.

The trail had taken them up a narrow valley that pointed them back toward the Beartooth mountains, then made a turn around a lone timber topped butte that was straddled by two creeks that came from the high mountains. After the turn to the north, they followed the creek about two miles and the trail turned back to the west pointing into the black timbered mountains. They stripped the gear from the horses, let them have a good roll then rubbed them down with hands full of dry grass before letting them stretch out on the patch of grass beneath the aspen. The men rolled out blankets and stretched out, needing some rest. It had been a long day and they traveled a little over ten miles from the camp. The horses had been on the move constantly and deserved a longer rest than Gabe was wanting to give them, but he knew he had be patient with the horses, for without them, they would never find their women.

11 / Chase

Their prayer time was spent in the saddle, moonlight before them, stretching long shadows that danced on the mountains. It was a short night and neither man slept, but with the uncertainty of the chase and the raiders treatment of the captives, they started out after less than three hours.

"You know, If I'da knowed what havin' a wife was gonna mean, I might oughta not done it!" grumbled Ezra, as they let the horses have their heads to pick their own way in the shadowy canyon that nestled between the tall mountains.

"Don't know what you're fussin' about. Last time, when them Frenchies took 'em, you was with 'em and I had to come to the rescue all by my lonesome! But you know you wouldn't have it any other way, same as me. The women are a part of us now, we wouldn't be complete without 'em, and I sure don't wanna go back to your cookin'!" answered Gabe. Although he fussed about it, he was glad Ezra rode with him, the two had developed a way about them that defied description, but in the heat of battle, they were like two parts of a whole, each anticipating what the other would do or where they would be in the fight. But it was more than just what the two of them shared, the women completed them and gave them purpose. No longer just a couple friends sharing an adventure, they were discovering and exploring new territory and that knowledge would be useful not just to themselves, but to the many others that would come after them. And if they could make the relationship between white men and natives a friendly one, it would be better for both.

***

The trail of the raiders stayed in the bottom of the cut between the crags, holding to the willows and alders, occasionally rising on a shoulder and cutting through the scrub oak brush. The valley bore due west, the north star settling on the mountain top like a new wick in a store-bought lamp. Black timber climbed on the south side and steep bald face limestone slopes on the north, were often dimpled by random juniper. The trail steadily climbed to the higher reaches, winding through willows and aspen, then passing through the stately ponderosa and spruce. Standing like a lone sentry at the end of the cut rose a single dome topped ridge, splitting the forks of the small run-off creek and guarding the dividing ridge behind. The trail followed the south fork through the timber to make its way around the sentry butte, but they were brought up short as it rose steeply to a saddle between the mountains. It was obvious this was an avalanche chute in the spring, but now with all the snow nothing more than a memory, the game trail showed as a thin line that switched back on itself as it bent onto the north slope before coming back to cross over the pass.

As they neared the crest, Gabe reined up and stepped down. He handed Ebony's reins to Ezra, slipped the scope from the saddlebags and walked across the bald slope the last quarter mile to the long saddle crossing. Ezra stepped down, stretched and stood in the shadow of a black fir that masked his presence in the dim fading moonlight. The big moon was hanging in the western sky, just above the crest of the crossing and behind him, the thin grey line of early morning was dimming the lanterns of the night sky.

Gabe walked back with the morning light stretching his shadow behind him, although his stride showed no haste, his long legs covered the ground quickly. "Wide long valley, pretty clear. Saw the light of a fire four, five miles down, big flat. Might be them."

He took the reins, swung aboard and gigged Ebony to take the trail to cross the saddle. Once crested, the timber on the far side gave more than ample cover. They faced a soft but cold wind that whistled up the valley, rattling the quakies that shook their leaves at the passersby as an old maid schoolteacher scolding them for being out of place. The trail moved from the dry creek bottom into the aspen groves, and back to the scrub oak. The steep mountain slopes that shouldered the left of the canyon were thick with black timber, while the lesser slopes on the right showed juniper and piñon like freckles on a barefoot redheaded boy. But the route stayed in the cover of terrain or timber as it wound its way to the lower climes.

"The fire I saw was at the edge of the wide meadow in the flat yonder," stated Gabe as he pointed through the trees that stretched to catch the morning sun bending its rays to the valley bottom. The two men were wending their way through the trees to the top of a finger ridge that offered a bit of a promontory for a scout of the valley. Once atop, they tethered the horses in the trees and worked to the point and crawled under the long branches of a fir and belly-down, stretched out the scope to survey the area.

"There! Just below that first flat, at the edge of the trees!" Declared Gabe, twisting the scope for clarity, trying to see more. "They're not movin' fast, too far to make out anybody, several are doubled up and that'll slow 'em down, but there's a bunch. Reckon, close to twenty warriors, but hard to tell from here." He lifted the scope toward the end of the valley, searched for sign of a trail, then twisted around to look at their back trail. "Here comes Shoots and the others." He handed the scope to Ezra, stood and shaded his eyes for a broader view, thinking, calculating, considering. He looked back up the valley toward the approaching Shoshone and Bannock, then down the valley at the retreating Blackfoot and their captives.

"Look! Look!" he declared, pointing and insisting Ezra look where he indicated. "If I cross over this ridge behind us, I might get ahead of 'em and stop 'em. If you hotfoot it back to Shoots and get him to come at a run, you can come behind 'em and we'll get 'em 'fore they get outta this valley."

Ezra looked where Gabe indicated, "You sure the trail bends around that point?" He was looking at the end of the ridge and the end of the valley. It appeared the ridge dead-ended into the line of smaller mountains that came from the others to the south, making a mountainous ridge that blocked the valley where they stood.

"Yeah. See, there's a stream that comes from that canyon there," he pointed to their left where a cut in the mountains held a runoff stream that flowed from the high mountains. "And it follows this ridge beside us to the end of the valley, then bends around that point. Now, there's either a mighty big lake that catches all that water, or that river keeps flowing and that's where that bunch of Blackfoot are headin'," explained Gabe.

"How you gonna stop 'em? That's a good-sized bunch!"

"You know me, I'll think of sumpin'," answered Gabe, going back to the horses. He looked at the ridge, picking out a possible crossing, and swung aboard Ebony. He looked down at Ezra, "Get a move on. If I stop 'em, I want you behind 'em."

"All right, I'm goin', you just mind your manners. Won't do no good to rescue the women if some Blackfoot has your scalp hangin' from his belt."

***

"Big Snake, you and one, go!" The swift motion sent the warrior and the one beside him off at run to serve as advance scouts. "Two Bulls, you and one, go!" Two more rode off swiftly to serve as guards behind the band of Niitsitapi raiders. The leader that ordered the others was A'kow-muk-ai, *Feathers,* but was also known as Old Swan. He was a young warrior but proven by his deeds on other raids. He had counted coup on war leaders of the Gros Ventre, Crow, and Shoshone. Stolen horses from Arapaho and Shoshone, taken captives from Assiniboine and Bannock, and now from the Shoshone. With eighteen warriors, they had taken the village and captured a dozen women and young people, only losing two warriors in the fight. Now they were two days from their village and he and his men would be welcomed with great honor and a feast.

He looked at the woman who rode beside him. Her hands were bound at her waist and a rawhide thong was around her throat with the end held in his hand. He jerked at the thong, making her look at him, "You will be my second wife! My woman has been whining for help, she says I ask too much. Now you will help her and serve me!" he laughed at her scowling expression. He did not know if she understood his language and he made no attempt to speak in Shoshone, although he knew a little of their tongue, but he felt it unnecessary. She would have to learn his language to understand whatever she was told, and the longer it took the more beatings she would have to bear.

Grey Dove glared at her captor, choosing to remain silent, although she understood what he said, having gained knowledge of the language of the Piegan Blackfoot when one of their young warriors had been a captive in her village. She looked back at the other captives and felt all alone. They had not been with the band long enough to make friends with the other women. She and her sister, Otter, had been too busy with their own chores and the needs of their men to spend any time with the others, and now she was alone among strangers and captors. But she was certain Ezra would come for her. Had not Gabe rescued them before when the French Coureur des bois had taken them? And Ezra would do no less. No matter how long it would take, he would come for her, she was certain of that. But she had to stay alive and she could not be this man's wife like he said, she already had a man and could not go to another. She sighed heavily, thinking, trying to think of some way to get free and run back to Ezra. Somehow, she must do whatever she could to be free. But for now, at least, she was riding.

12 / Cutoff

Gabe wheeled Ebony around to take the slope behind them. The valley below was bordered on the north side by a timbered ridge that stretched the length of the valley, about four miles, and rose at least twelve hundred feet above the valley floor. Ebony felt the urgency of his rider and eagerly took to the trees, wending his way through the spruce and fir that spread their branches in low swooping arcs. Gabe chuckled as he was reminded of the high waisted and long flowing dresses the women wore to the social events of the year. He remembered the powdered wigs of the women and chuckled again as the trees made him think of the dresses and the high-country glaciers that topped the mountains of the powdered wigs. He shook his head at the thought and told himself *this* was his kind of high society 'doins,' climbing through the timber to top out on a mountain ridge and go meet the neighbors with a proper greeting.

As they crested the knoll, Gabe paused, looking to the draw below and followed it uphill to the crest of the tall mountain that anchored the long ridge. Judging that to be their best route, he gigged Ebony down the hill to the draw. Once at the bottom, he turned to follow the gravelly dry bed as it came from on high. He knew water always took the path of least resistance and knew this would take him near the crest of the ridge, but he was soon disappointed. The run-off had cut its way from the avalanche chute and swung wide of the ridge. He reined up, searched the slope for a route then spoke to Ebony, "Maybe we can pick our way across the face of that slope and get over the top." He sat upright, gigged the black forward and let him pick his own path through the trees across the steep slope. Gabe put all his weight in the uphill side stirrup, leaning into the hill, watching every step Ebony took. The stallion chose a path that took them below a pocket of shale but brought them to a halt at an insurmountable rise, too steep to assault. Gabe stepped down on the high side, searching the slope for a possible route, then moved in front of the black, and took the lead, rein in hand as he grabbed at a long branch of a leaning fir, pushed his way around by digging in his heels and pushing the dirt down to make a bit of a path as he passed the tree. Once around, he tugged on the rein, "C'mon boy, you can do it," and with steady pressure, urged Ebony closer.

Gabe chose what he thought was the only possible path, and started picking his way, bending Ebony around to follow as they cut back toward the top of the ridge. Each step was measured, calculated and taken slowly and carefully. One slip on this steep slope could end up with both of them at the bottom, which was now almost a thousand feet below. Gabe stood beside Ebony's head, the slope so steep, his hip was even with the horse's head. He looked at what he thought would be a possible route, but what he thought might be possible for him, might not be stable enough for Ebony. He looked at the big horse, put his arm over his neck and spoke, "Boy, I'm gonna let you pick your own way. I'll start out, but you need to come as you can." He stroked the big black's neck, ran his fingers through his mane, then hung the rein over Ebony's neck and started out. Each step, the dirt slid beneath him, several times he stumbled, catching himself with the uphill arm, then continuing. He looked back to see Ebony watching, then took several more steps, paused, when suddenly Ebony was following. The long-legged black picked his steps but when he came alongside Gabe, he kept going, just downhill from his friend, but close enough to touch. As he passed, Gabe grabbed the tail end of the tie string that held his bedroll, and hung on, stumbling beside the black, as he lunged and dug his way to the crest of the ridge.

Once atop the ridge, they stopped for a breather and to pick a route to the bottom. He looked west down the long ridge, saw the end that abutted up to the opposite range and the riverbed that came from the valley. He grinned, relieved that he was right in what he guessed was the probable route of the raiders. He looked along the base of the ridge, saw the unusual formation that looked like lines drawn across the finger ridges and marked by the lines of timber. Then a quick search below them showed the run-off bed that would be the quickest route to the bottom. He swung aboard Ebony, pointed him to the draw below, "Let's go, boy! We've gotta beat 'em to the end o' this here ridge!"

As Ebony took the first long stride off the crest, Gabe leaned way back over the cantle of his saddle, drove his feet deep in the stirrups and let Ebony have his head. Several stiff-legged lunges brought the horse to the bottom of the draw and the dry run-off creek. With a few side-steps to get his balance, the big black took to the sandy bottom and started down the creek bed faster than Gabe would have liked, but he hung on and lay low on the stallion's neck, the black mane slapping him in the face. Although it seemed like ten, it was just over a mile and they broke from the timber. Gabe reined up, stepped down and caught his breath. He walked a short distance, leading Ebony, who was breathing heavy but confident in his steps. Once both horse and rider were breathing regular, Gabe stepped back aboard and kicked Ebony to a canter, then a gallop, as they followed a creek-side trail that pointed toward the river that came from the valley. From high on the ridge, he had spotted this wide arroyo and knew it would be their route to cut-off the escape of the raiders.

The creek he followed soon cleared the many finger ridges that came from the timbered ridge he crossed earlier. He pointed the black away from the creek to cut across a wide grassy swale to get to the river from the canyon. He spotted a bald ridge that shouldered the river, turned his big black to mount the promontory and once atop, slipped to the ground, scope in hand and with one knee on the ground, he stretched out the scope to find the raiders. He was about a half mile from the mouth of the canyon, a mile and a half uphill from the confluence of the two streams. But the canyon's river bent around a timbered point that came from the east side and obscured his view into the canyon. He looked across the river at the far hills and spotted one that shouldered into the valley bottom would probably afford him a view up-river. He thought for a moment but ruled out crossing the river bottom and possibly exposing himself to the raiders. Yet where he sat, the valley was about a mile wide and offered nothing that would be suitable for an ambush that would stop the raiders.

He scanned the valley bottom quickly, "There!" he declared to himself. "That same point!" The ridge that pushed into the valley and cut off his view of the upper end, was also timbered and rocky, narrowing the valley to no more than two hundred yards. "That'll do!" he declared as he stepped back aboard his black, slipping the cased scope into the saddle bags. "But," he started as he leaned down to stroke Ebony's neck, "we've got to get there before they do! Think you can do it? I think you can! Let's go!" he said as he slapped leather and heels to the big stallion.

Ebony launched them off the slight ridge in one long jump, startling Gabe and making him grab at the pommel. When the horse hit the ground, he was off at a full run, staying wide of the brush and trees by the river, head stretched out, mane and tail flying, as he aimed for the timber covered finger that fell in a heap from high above and rooted itself in a rock pile at its base. Within moments, the two miles had been put behind them and Gabe reined the black up a bit of a shoulder that held a narrow tree-filled basin. He dropped to the ground, loosened the girth of the black and let him drop his face into the grass at his feet.

He stripped his weapons from the saddle, jamming both saddle pistols into his belt with the Bailes over/ under pistol. He brought out the Mongol bow, sat down and bent it toward him to nock the string. He stood, hung the quiver at his belt beside the tomahawk, felt at his back for the knives and reassured, slipped the Ferguson rifle from the scabbard. He walked to the line of rock that marked the edge of the shoulder. Along the edge were several chokecherry bushes and some scrub oak. In the narrow basin behind him was a thick grove of aspen, mature trees that were a foot and more in diameter and standing twenty plus feet high. The leaves twisted and turned in the slight mountain breeze that came down the valley, rattling enough to mask any sound he might make. It was good cover and he settled down to plan his ambush.

His position was about a hundred twenty feet above the canyon floor and directly below him the river pushed against the base of the shoulder. The waterway twisted its way down the valley and bent back on itself time and again. Upstream of his position, the river cascaded down through a narrow cut, shouldered on both sides by ridges that pushed together and forced the trail to high ground on a narrow butte. The trail dropped off the high ground and came back alongside the river, but when the stream came to the shoulder where Gabe sat, the trail crossed to the other side and was in open ground that offered nothing for cover. When the raiders were in that flat, they would be under his fire with both the bow and rifle, and if they chose to charge his position, his pistols would come into play. Gabe nodded as he pictured the action, and his movements in all possibilities of the raiders' response to his attack. He leaned back and began checking each of his weapons, while he waited their approach.

13 / Battle

Once out of the trees, the band of warriors with Shoots Running Buffalo and Ezra kicked their mounts up to a canter. The trail of the raiders was clear as it followed the river in the valley bottom, with as many as thirty horses, their own plus those of the captives, the ground was well trodden and turned. But the raiders were four or five miles ahead and it would be hard to cut the lead without overly tiring the horses. Although these were mountain bred horses, and they had greater stamina than most, it was necessary to pace them to avoid breaking their wind. Horses would respond to their riders beyond the measure of their ability, always striving to do whatever was bidden. But any man that valued his horse would give him the best of care, knowing that a man without a horse in this country would considerably lessen his chance of survival.

After a mile at a canter, they dropped back to a walk, giving the horses a breather. Shoots slid to the ground and walked alongside his mount, his warriors following his example. As Ezra walked beside his bay, he hung his possibles pouch on the saddle horn, stuffed his pistol in the pommel, and lay his war club across his bedroll. He lifted his shirt over his head, and lay it across the seat of his saddle, then hung the war club between his shoulders, and replaced the other weapons in his belt. He rolled his shoulders back, flexing his muscles, and breathing deep. He paid little attention to the others who were surprised to see him shirtless, like they themselves were most often, but were impressed with the deep chested man whose torso and back muscles rippled with his moves. His shoulders and arms bulged as he flexed, twisting at his waist and breathing deep. The others watched, knowing he was preparing for the fight and that his name, Black Buffalo, suited this man that showed the image of a buffalo by his size and build. And most thought they were glad they would not have to fight him, as they would sooner try to wrestle a bull buffalo to the ground one handed. Then when he snatched his war club from behind his back and swung it in an arc before him, one handed, then with both arms, it was obvious that anyone or anything that felt a blow from this man and his club would not survive.

Shoots motioned to the others and everyone swung back aboard their horses and he slapped legs to kick them up to a canter again. But Ezra grew impatient, thinking only of Dove and what she might be suffering, and he turned to Shoots, "I'm going to scout ahead!" and without waiting for a response, took off at a full gallop in pursuit of the raiders.

***

Two Bulls and his fellow Blackfoot had dropped behind the band of raiders and took up a position of cover to watch their back-trail. They had tethered their horses back in the trees that stood on the bank of the creek in the valley bottom, and they sat on an upthrust of rocks at the edge of the trees. They had been watching for most of an hour and were not expecting any pursuit from the defeated Shoshone, but the sudden sound of beating hooves brought them up from behind their cover. They saw a lone rider, lying low on the neck of his horse and coming at a full run toward them. Both men quickly nocked arrows and stepped forward, trying for a clear shot at the running horse. They let arrows fly, but the rider had dropped to the far side of his mount and the arrows flew harmlessly overhead.

He had expected to find at least one Blackfoot on rear guard, so when Ezra saw the movement at the stack of rocks, he slid to the far side of his horse and kept going at a run. He couldn't risk a shot with either rifle or pistol that would alarm the band of raiders. As he drew nearer, he rose up, snatched his war club from his back and charged directly at the two men. They had not expected one man to charge them and they were frantically nocking arrows for another shot, but Ezra screamed his war cry and the men started to dive for cover, but the war club swung down, striking the first warrior with the blade at the base of his neck, knocking him to the ground, blood spurting wildly over the rocks as he grabbed at his neck. Ezra wheeled the bay around and charged at the second man, ducking just as an arrow tugged at the rawhide strap holding his possibles bag. Another swing of the war club and the second warrior dropped to the ground, the top of his head caved in and bleeding. With a quick glance at the fallen men, Ezra turned away and took to the trail again.

As the trail topped a slight rise, Ezra looked toward the valley's end and saw the last of the band of warriors disappear around the bend. He was quickly closing the gap, but there were too many for one man to attack, but he knew Gabe would be somewhere ahead. He would have to pace his pursuit to be there when Gabe struck. Then, with the surprise of the ambush, perhaps he could get to the captives and free Dove and Otter.

***

At first sight of the band of raiders cresting the low rise beyond the cascades of the river, Gabe hunkered down, keeping his telescope on the bunch, searching for the captives and any sight of his Otter. But the leaders of the band were all Blackfoot, but the one man had a woman in tow with a neck loop, and as he watched, he recognized the woman as Grey Dove, Ezra's woman. Gabe had formulated a bit of a plan, but his actions would be determined by the raiders, what route they would take, where they would be bunched, and more.

Suddenly the band came to a halt when two warriors rode up to the leader. They came from the other side of the ridge where Gabe lay, and he was surprised to see them. Maybe they had seen him and were reporting his position to the leader. Gabe reached for one of the two whistler arrows he had lain on the rock beside him but kept the scope on the leader. The scouts were talking and gesticulating, but there didn't seem to be any alarm among the group in the lead. When the leader nodded, then motioned, the two scouts backed their mounts away to let the others pass, probably to fall in after the leaders.

Gabe grinned, *Good, now if they just cross over the river there . . .* he watched as the band came off the edge of the low mesa dropping down to the level of the river. The winding stream had come from the cascades, bent back on itself, forming a long peninsula that pointed toward the far side mountains, but the obvious crossing was where the trail took to the water at a break in the willows, and the leader with Dove in tow, started into the shallow crossing.

Gabe glanced at his placement of his weapons back along the natural breastwork that lined the edge of the abutment where he waited. He looked below him and across the narrows, calculating the far edge was at the limit of both rifle and bow, just less than four hundred yards. He breathed deep, nocked the first of the two whistler arrows and waited for the band to draw near. As he watched, he saw most of the warriors were at the front of the cavalcade, followed by the captives and a few warriors on either side, and a rear guard behind the captives of three, maybe four warriors. He wanted to try to separate the band at the front from the captives, freeing him to make his assault without concern for the captives, all that is, except for Dove.

As he watched, the band followed the primary and easier trail that was close to the stream and would bring them just below his position, although there was another trail that held to the base of the far mountain, they made the obvious choice, as Gabe had hoped. As the leader came closer to the stream, the captives were just entering the little meadow and Gabe brought the Mongol bow to full draw, brought his aim high, and loosed the arrow. As it took flight, he grabbed the second whistler, waited just a moment as he saw the first reaction of those below, and loosed the second arrow to fly over their heads before descending to strike.

The high-pitched scream of the arrows startled the

Blackfoot as they searched the sky for the cause, and the second scream came on the tail of the first, causing the alarm to spread and horses, with their riders showing panic and jerking on the reins and twisting about, began to spook. When Dove heard the first arrow, she added her scream to the pandemonium, then shouted to the leader of the Blackfoot, in his own language, "Aiiieee! It is the claw of Spirit Bear! He will bring death on all of you! Black Buffalo will soon be among you and none can stand before him!"

A scream came from behind them as the first arrow plummeted from the sky as the warriors looked at the bright sun overhead searching for the screaming phantom as the first arrow plunged into the upper chest of a warrior, the arrowhead exiting his lower back. The second arrow impaled itself in the rump of a horse that reared up and bucked off its rider before it took off at a run, the arrow flopping and chirping as the horse tried to outrun what was buried deep in its muscular hip. Other horses became skittish as their riders fought to bring them under control and Gabe took advantage of the confusion. He took careful aim at the leaders, sent two more arrows, both taking their targets in the chest and unseating them.

Gabe lay his bow down, scampered to where his rifle lay and lifted it to take aim at the man who still held the tether of Dove, he squeezed off his shot and the boom racketed off the far rock face, echoing up the valley. The blast had startled the Blackfoot, and Old Swan slid to the ground. The weapon of white men was still a rarity in this part of the world, and the explosion of powder was almost as effective as the bullets themselves, rattling the confidence of the warriors that bragged about fearing nothing, but now all were frightened as one man brought death to so many. Then within seconds, warriors had raced their horses to the edge of the stream, dropped to the ground, seeking cover behind the willows. But there were still others that offered ample target and Gabe quickly reloaded the rifle, took aim and dropped another. He went back to his bow, spotted a target nearer the captives and far beyond the range of any of the bows of the Blackfoot, and with careful aim, he sent a long black arrow to impale itself in the neck of one of the warriors that stood before the captives. Two others saw him fall, and searched for the shooter, but there was no one within the usual range of a bow.

Gabe picked a target that showed his back behind the willows and quickly sent an arrow to take the man down, and with a scream, the man rose, twisting to grab at the arrow, and fell into the brush before him. Gabe returned to his rifle, having already re-loaded before he lay it down, but when he saw two warriors starting across the stream, he moved to the next position and picked up his saddle pistol, cocked it and brought it to bear on the first of the waders, then dropped the hammer and the pistol bucked and roared, the smoke from the muzzle briefly blocking Gabe's view of the warrior, but he saw the man splash face first in the stream. He cocked the second hammer, took aim at the second warrior, who had paused when his companion was hit and searched the bluff before him, but just as he spotted movement, the lead ball took him in the neck and he swam with his fellow warrior, face down with the current.

A commotion toward the rear of the band caught Gabe's attention, and he saw the blackness of Ezra, swinging his war club, side to side, as he waded into the warriors near the captives. Gabe grinned, then looked below for another target. He was reloading the pistol by feel, easily going through each step without taking his eyes off the pandemonium below him. When another man tried breaking through the brush, Gabe picked up the second pistol and stopped him with a big piece of lead that shattered bone and meat as it plowed through the man's chest. Gabe kept his watch, finished reloading and returned to his bow.

He knew the Blackfoot were confused as to how many were attacking. With arrows and gunshots coming from different positions, they were unable to determine who or how many were attacking. Then war cries and screams came from behind the captives, and from both sides of the cascades, the band of Shoshone charged into the melee.

14 / Rescue

The leader, known as Feathers or Old Swan, had taken a bullet in his shoulder and was knocked from his horse, but when the others made for the brush at the riverside, he too crawled for cover. It was Big Snake that reached out and drew his leader closer to the brush and asked, "What are we to do?"

"How many are there?" asked Feathers, nodding toward the bluff.

"Do not know. Some with bows, some with white man's guns, five, six, or more."

"But others attack there," added Feathers, pointing toward the rear of their band where the captives had been herded near the brush.

"This one shoots there!" declared Big Snake. Feathers scowled at him, "No man can shoot arrows that far!"

"I saw!"

"No, you are wrong. There must be others!" He leaned

to the side to try to see the end of the cascades where the rest of his warriors and the captives had taken cover. It was then he saw another warrior, painted black, attacking his warriors at the end of his band. He remembered the scream of the woman at his side when she said one named Black Buffalo would come among them and kill many. He looked around for the woman, but she was not to be seen. He looked among the bushes, saw only three other warriors besides Big Snake and himself, then glowered at Big Snake. "Attack there!" pointing to the bluff.

"But, three have tried, all are dead!" complained Big Snake, looking at the other warriors huddled behind the brush.

Feathers looked around, heard screams coming from those with the captives, glared at Big Snake, "Get our horses! We will go!"

Snake looked at his leader, saw the horses milling nearby, and started crawling beside the brush toward the animals. He spotted the dun that was ridden by Feathers, grabbed the trailing reins and stepped behind the horse, using it for a shield from the shooters on the bluff. He led it close to his own horse, and walking between them, led them to the wounded leader. Feathers crawled toward the horses, then from between them, let Big Snake lift him aboard. Then Snake swung aboard his and the two men, laying low on their horses' necks, dug heels to the horses' ribs and started out of the canyon on a run.

***

Gabe watched one man crawl behind the bushes, going for the horses, but he chose not to shoot. He wasn't here to kill, but to rescue, and as long as they were not taking any captives, he would let them flee. The man soon caught one horse, then the second, and Gabe watched as the first man helped the other, and when they were mounted, they left without so much as a glance back at the others.

The turmoil was lessening, and the Shoshone were approaching the remaining few by the brush below Gabe's position. He knew there were only two or three left alive and they would soon be overtaken by the Shoshone. He gathered up his weapons, walked back to where Ebony was tethered and put the pistols in the holsters, the Ferguson in the scabbard, and once the Mongol bow was encased, he hung the case beneath the left fender of the saddle. He checked the load of his belt pistol, replaced it and started off the bluff to join the others and find Pale Otter.

Dove saw Gabe come off the bluff, and with a quick glance around, she walked from the brush to greet him. Gabe rode beside her, reached down and lifted her up behind him. As she settled on the bedroll, her hands at Gabe's side, he turned and asked, "Where's Otter?"

Dove caught her breath, leaned to the side to look at Gabe, "She is not here! She was not taken!"

Gabe twisted around to look at her, "What do you mean, she's not here?"

"She was gone when the Blackfoot attacked. She was with Moon Walker."

"Moon Walker? He was at the camp?" asked Gabe, looking from Dove to the group of captives and back. He saw Ezra walking toward him and gigged the black forward. Ezra saw him coming, saw Dove lean around him and started running to meet them. When they neared, Gabe reined up and Dove slid down, caught before her feet touched the ground in the arms of Ezra, bloody from the toe to toe battle he had waged with the Blackfoot. Gabe stepped down, dropped Ebony's reins to ground tie the stallion and started toward the captives, many already embracing their men. He walked among them, searching, hoping Dove was wrong and that he would find Otter, but she was not with the others. He turned back, started toward Ezra and Dove who stood arms around one another watching him.

Ezra looked at him, "She told me."

Gabe looked at Dove again, "Why did she go with Moon Walker?"

"He insisted they talk. She did not want to go but thought that was the only way to get rid of him." She saw the claw necklace at his throat, "She made that as a surprise for you and wanted to give it to you as soon as you came back from the scout."

"Did he force her? Take her?"

"No, but he demanded she go. He said it was just to talk. But I know he did not like that she was with you. He had tried to get our father to give her to him, but he would not. Otter was willing, but that was before you came. She is happy with you and does not want to be with Moon Walker. But when the Blackfoot came, they were gone. I do not know where they were, but I did not see them when the Blackfoot were taking all the women."

"Where would he take her?" asked Gabe, his frustration showing as he bit off his words.

"Maybe to his band, they are the *Boho'inee*. They are a mixed band, like these," she nodded to the other captives. "Shoots Buffalo would know where they go for the summer hunt."

Gabe dropped his gaze, shook his head and lifted his eyes to the mouth of the canyon. To find one man in this vast country was a daunting task, if not impossible. But Otter needed him to find her, to save her from what could be a life of misery and even torture for a man like Moon Walker that had borne the anger and vehemence that drove him to take her from her people, from her mate, from her sister, was capable of anything, anything that suited his twisted idea of vengeance or retribution. He had been spurned by Otter's family and he believed by Otter herself, and he would only be concerned with what he felt was due him, punishment and reprisal. But the fact he had taken Otter instead of meeting Gabe and fighting for her told much about the man. He was the kind that would sneak around to get his way, never confronting his opponent but striking in the dark or when his adversary was absent or could not defend himself or keep what was rightfully his.

With a cursory glance to Ezra and Dove, Gabe turned away to seek out Shoots. The Shoshone leader looked up as Gabe approached and stood to greet Gabe with a broad smile. "You have done much. My warriors could not count the number that fell under your weapons. There were at least one hand that fell, perhaps others."

Gabe came closer, nodded, then asked, "Where would Moon Walker go?"

"Moon Walker? He was not here. Why do you seek him?" asked Shoots, frowning.

"He came to the village before the Blackfoot attacked and took my woman, Pale Otter."

Shoots stepped back, scowling as he looked at Gabe, "You know this how?"

"Her sister, Grey Dove," nodding in her direction, "told me Moon Walker came into the camp and took her away before the attack by the Blackfoot. They did not return and there were tracks leading away from the camp."

Shoots gritted his teeth, the muscles in his cheeks

showing his effort to stay his anger. He looked at Gabe, "It is a bad thing he does. What will you do?"

"Go after him, of course. But I'm not sure whether to track him or try to find his village before he gets there. That's why I need to know where they would be found."

Shoots motioned for Gabe to follow him to the edge of the meadow where a line of boulders offered solitude and seating. He motioned for Gabe to be seated and began, "Moon Walker claimed to be a part of the village because his mother's mother was the sister of Owitze, our chief. Walker was accepted because he was a war leader with his people, the *Boho'inee*. They are known as the Sage Grass people and they camp beyond the Yellowstone where the three rivers meet. That is the beginning of the river the whites call Missouri.

"Few of our people liked Walker, but he was a good fighter and hunter. When he wanted a woman, none were willing, for he was known to beat his women. None of the fathers would let him take their daughters and he was always angry. We expected him to leave when the village broke up for the summer hunt. None of the families asked him to join them, but there were two or three warriors that followed him. If he went back to his village, they would be in the land of three rivers. But . . ." he shrugged, implying that there was no certainty where he would be found.

Gabe breathed heavily, kicked at a small stone at his feet, shook his head and looked at Shoots, "Any ideas?"

"Will you go alone, or will your friend go with you?"

"I'll be goin' alone. He needs to take care of his woman. They will probably return to her village in the Wind River range."

"Then remember, Moon Walker is not a man to be trusted. He will not meet you like a true warrior and he will not treat your woman as he should. If he leaves a clear trail, question it, for he could set an ambush. And if you fight him, beware, he is a good fighter, but he knows many ways to fight and you cannot trust him." Gabe stood, reached out to shake and the two men clasped forearms in the manner of the Indian, then parted.

***

When he returned to Ezra, he looked at his friend, and said, "You've got a woman to care for, I think it best if you return to her village with her."

Ezra frowned, "You're not goin' after Moon Walker alone?!"

"He is one man. And you must care for Grey Dove, she has been through a lot and you can't ask her to do more. And to leave her behind, no, you can't do that," answered Gabe. "Besides, I'll probably catch up with 'em real soon and maybe we'll even beat you back to the village." He reached out and grabbed Ezra's hand, placed his other hand on his friend's shoulder and drew him close. The two friends embraced, then separated.

15 / Trail

He caught the steeldust mustang from the captive herd, brought her back to where the others waited and began rigging her for packing. Without the packsaddles and panniers, Gabe could only fashion a blanket and a wide strip of buckskin into a bundle and latigo. He put his bedroll, that had been stuffed with what supplies they salvaged from the burnt tipi at the last camp, into the bundle and strapped it down. Ezra watched as his friend made ready for his foray into the mountains after his captured bride.

"I still think we should go with you!" declared Ezra as he stood near Gabe, watching him strap things down.

"I know we've been together all this time and never done anything without the other, but it's bad 'nuff we lost one wife, and if anything were to happen to Dove neither one of us could handle it. I'll travel faster and farther by my lonesome. This boy," he said as he patted Ebony on the neck, "can stretch out faster and last longer than most so . . ."

"The way I figger it, he's gonna have about four, maybe five days headstart on you. It took us two days comin' here from the camp, and two days back. Plus he had all day that first day 'fore we got back from the scout. That's gonna be hard for any horse to make up," surmised Ezra.

"All the more reason for me to get a move on and not waste any more time," added Gabe, swinging up into the saddle. He reached down and shook Ezra's hand, looked to Dove and said, "You take care of this man!"

Dove smiled, nodded and stepped beside Ezra, taking his arm in hers, pulling herself close. Both looked up at Gabe then watched him start from the canyon at a canter, turning east to follow the lower trail back to the valley of the Stillwater River to pick up the trail at the abandoned campsite. He took to the same path he made when coming off the long timber covered mountain ridge, followed it to the point where he crossed over, then swung to the north a couple miles to go around a high thin mountain ridge that pushed out into the valley of rugged foothills. They climbed to surmount the saddle and dropped into the long valley that stretched the length of the mountains. Another saddle crossing and they dropped into the creek bottom that separated the mountain shoulders from the ragged and scarred foothills.

The sun was tucked behind the mountains and the mountain shadows stretched toward the foothills when Gabe came to the tracks made by the Shoshone as they pursued the Blackfoot. This was the same timber topped butte that marked the entrance to the valley taken by Gabe and Ezra when they were trailing the raiders. The terrain they covered had dictated the pace they moved and for the last couple of miles he had kept Ebony at a canter, but when he spotted the familiar trail, he knew he was nearing the site of the abandoned camp and he pulled Ebony back to a walk.

Gabe leaned forward on the cantle, looking around at the mountains in the fading light of dusk, and muttered a quick prayer for God to give him the sight and stamina that would be needed in this long chase. He also asked for Otter's safety, but for some reason he paused as he said that, thinking of what Shoots had said about Moon Walker and his treatment of women. He breathed deep, shook his head as he gritted his teeth and balled his hands into fists. He beat one fist into his thigh, angry at himself for being so careless to leave Otter unprotected, or at least unprepared.

When they came to the remains of the camp, several carrion eaters scattered. Crows, turkey vultures, and magpies took flight, a pair of coyotes scampered, and a badger skulked away. Although the bodies of the Shoshone and Bannock had been cared for, the remains of the Blackfoot warriors and a couple horses were left where they lay, enticing the clean-up crew of the wilderness. Other rodents were picking over the partially burned remains of winter stores that had been left behind in the ashes, and all scattered as Gabe rode through the campsite. He went to the place where the tripod of partially burnt poles of their hide lodge still stood. He paused, looking down at the picked over pile, then moved into the thin line of trees at the river's edge and stepped down.

After stripping the gear from both horses, he let them roll in the dirt, take a long drink from river's edge, then rubbed them both down with handfuls of dry grass. He picketed them on long tethers, then rolled out his blankets. He was too tired to bother with a fire and took some pemmican and walked to the edge of the river, letting the chuckling of the water as it moved over the rocks soothe him. His thoughts went to Otter, wondering where she was and how she was faring, and even as he chewed on the pemmican, he felt her presence, knowing her hands had prepared what he now ate. Her image danced before him, her long fringed wedding dress that shone white in the dim light, her smile that lifted his heart, and her long hair that he reached for, only to be disappointed as the image dissipated into the darkness.

He stood and walked back to his blankets, stretched out and with hands clasped behind his head, he looked at the darkening sky, watching as the lanterns were lit, thin touches of light that clustered to form the constellations, and the slowly brightening milky way that the Indians called the road to the other side. He closed his eyes and turned on his side, drawing the blanket over his shoulder, but as soon as he wiggled to a comfortable spot, his eyes opened, and he listened to the sounds of the varmints finishing what he had interrupted. The crunching of bone, tearing of hides, hissing and spitting as they fought over tidbits, did little to lull him to sleep, but his tired body finally relaxed, and he slept.

The moon was waxing full and hung high overhead when Gabe rolled from his blankets. He guessed it to be a couple hours past midnight as he mounted up, picked up the lead of the steeldust, and started up the canyon. He was unconcerned about finding the trail for this was the way they came through the mountains just days before and the trail was narrow and there were few places to exit the steep walled canyon. Although Ezra had calculated as many as five days that Moon Walker had on him, by making the miles he did on the first day already cut that down. As he thought about it, it would be most of one day when they were gone on the scout, then two days in the pursuit, but his return made that in one day. So, four days lead was what Moon Walker had and Gabe knew he could cut that down with his long-legged stallion and the mountain bred steeldust mustang.

The first possible cutoff was the same he and Ezra had taken when they took the bighorn, but a quick check of the only trail that took to the trees and the narrow canyon with the waterfall showed nothing. But his quick check of the waterfall route brought him high over the granite mound that formed the narrow canyon of the Stillwater and as he dropped from the trees, he spotted the tracks of two horses, three or more days old, moving up into the deep canyon. He grinned as he recognized the tracks of Otter's Blue Roan and he kicked the black into a canter as the canyon bottom opened enough for the wide trail.

He rounded the point of rocks and the valley opened to the wide grassy flats that carried the now slow-moving Stillwater. The trail stayed wide of the river and pointed due south between the majestic granite shoulders of the mountains that seemed to part for his passing. The river dropped over a series of cascades as it came from a higher valley and was joined by two smaller creeks, one from either side of the canyon, creeks that carried the late spring runoff of the last of the high mountain snow.

The tracks of Otter and Moon Walker turned suddenly and crossed the white-water creek that now was little more than twenty feet across. Gabe gigged Ebony across, paused as he lifted his eyes high above to see the rocky crags of the mountains. The one on his right rose to a thin point, made more impressive by the scarred face that told of time and weather worn stone that showed its age like the wrinkles of an old man. The peak on his left stood tall with moss and scrub oak holding to tenuous fissures and colored the face green. The mountains stood opposing one another but guarding the perilous passage from those unworthy or unable to meet the demands of the rugged Rockies.

From below, Gabe was dwarfed by the monstrous monoliths that dared him to enter the narrow defile and the whistling wind seemed to whisper a warning. He stood in his stirrups and could barely make out where the trail turned back to the south at the face of a crumbling cliff with a talus slope that slid to the creek bottom. He reached down and petted Ebony on his neck, "Well, I didn't figger this'd be easy. Let's go boy," and he gigged Ebony to the trail that shadowed the thin creek.

It was a steep climb up the first mile and a half to the point where the trail cut back at the face of the cliff. But what he hadn't seen from below, was the trail seemed to end at the base of a long cascading waterfall. He backed away from the stream, searching the sidewalls for any sign of the tracks of the horses of Walker and Otter. He had missed where they left the creek bottom and took to the talus slope below the cliff face. Now he saw where they had taken to the slide rock, worked across the smaller shale of the talus, then took a narrow shoulder to the crest above the falls. He sighed heavily, stepped down, and started up the slope. He tucked the rein into his belt at his back, freeing both hands for balance and more as he led the way across the treacherous slope.

When they came to the shale of the talus, the tracks of the others showed both digging deep and some sliding, so Gabe carefully picked each step, giving ample length to both the reins of Ebony and the lead of the steeldust. But where Gabe was cautious and fearful, sliding often, the horses appeared to have no trouble. They tested each step, took another, and carefully crossed the narrows. In short order they came to the crest and Gabe sat down, catching his breath as the horses casually grazed on the mountain grass.

The sure-footed horses made the rest of the ascent on the circuitous trail amidst the rocky escarpments with little difficulty. The bright moonlight revealed every crag and rock, but the trail was solid and soon took to the timber where the path was easier among the tall fir trees. The high country was dotted with deep blue lakes, although none were more than a half mile across or long. When they crested the trail, the flats held a lake surrounded by greenery that seemed out of place, but Gabe chose to give the horses a much-needed rest. He loosened the girths, ground tied them on the grass, and seated himself on a grassy mound to enjoy the warmth of the rising sun. The trail they had ascended pointed them west and appeared to keep that direction. He thought for a few moments and knew that he had traveled a long u-shaped path. When he left the others at the scene of the battle with the raiders, he had traveled back to the east, then south in the valley of the Stillwater, now back to the west through this trail. As Shoots had described the location of the land of the *Boho'inee*, he knew it was northwest of where they had the battle. Now it seemed Moon Walker was going back to the land of his people. But what did that mean? Was he taking the woman he now saw as his with him to his village? Or was he returning to the land of his family to regain his position as war leader, with or without a woman? But if his people knew what he had done, would they accept him back?

Gabe looked at the grazing horses, and spoke aloud, "Looks like we'll just have to catch up with him before he gets to his people! Don't want to have to fight the whole family!"

16 / Camp

They must have come in the night. Otter had not slept since she was taken from the village by Moon Walker and even though she was still bound to the tree, she had fallen into a deep sleep. But now there were two other warriors that talked with Moon Walker, gesturing toward her and arguing.

"You should kill her now! She will tell our people what you have done, and we will be banished!" proclaimed the one known as Porcupine. His name was He Who Eats Porcupine, but anyone that called him by his full name risked an attack by the big man. Although the name did more to describe his prickly nature and his rotund build, it had been given him as one who would eat anything, even a porcupine with all his quills.

The second warrior showed his agreement by his expression but chose to remain silent. Red Hawk was a proven warrior and chose to follow Moon Walker because he knew wherever this man went there would be fighting and he relished any fight, it was the only way to vent his anger and show his disgust for anyone who did not fight as he thought they should. He had no preference nor concern for whoever he did battle with, as long as he could shed blood and take scalps, believing those who chose to just count coup were cowards. It was better to take the life of your enemies so they could not fight again. Although both Red Hawk and Porcupine were Shoshone, they had left their band, the *Haivo·ika,* because their leader had chosen to be friendly with other tribes and their band had become known as Dove Eaters because of their timid ways. They met Moon Walker when they visited the *Tukkutikka* band of the Shoshone and Moon Walker had shown himself as a fighter against the Crow. When he chose to return to his people, the *Boho'inee,* they followed.

"She is my woman!" spat Moon Walker. "If I keep her, she will tend my lodge and be my woman! If she tries to tell my people anything, *then* I will kill her!"

Porcupine stepped back, looked at the woman tied to the tree, "What kind of woman is she that you have to bind her to a tree? Are you not man enough to handle her?"

Moon Walker lunged toward the bigger man, hitting him on the chest with both hands, knocking him back. As he stumbled to catch his balance, Walker slipped his knife from the sheath at his waist and brought it to Porcupine's throat, "I will slit your throat before I kill her! She is of more use to me than you!"

Porcupine caught his balance and stood wide-eyed as he looked down at Walker, fearing to move with the knife at his throat. His nostrils flared and he snarled, "You do as you want! She is not my worry!"

Walker stepped back and sheathed his knife, looked from Porcupine to Red Hawk and said, "We will go to the village of my people, the *Boho'inee.* I will be the war leader and we will fight together!"

"Who? Who do we fight?" demanded Red Hawk, stepping closer, his lip curling and his eyes glaring.

"The Blackfoot! They attacked the camp where I took her! They should be taken and destroyed! And the Salish! They have attacked my people and we can take women and horses from them!"

"Aiiieeee!" screamed Red Hawk, brandishing his scalping knife. "I will take many scalps from the Black-foot! Then they will know the blade of Red Hawk! And women! Women from the Salish!" he cackled his glee, looked at Porcupine and added, "Even Porcupine should have a woman from the Salish!"

Both Porcupine and Moon Walker laughed at the antics of Red Hawk, and Walker glanced at Otter, snarled, "If she does not do as I say, she will be left behind, and I too will take a woman from the Salish!"

Moon Walker and Otter had ridden hard for two

days and most of two nights, all to reach the meeting site on the Yellowstone River. Now that the other warriors had joined them she was concerned about what they would do next. She looked across the river hoping to see Gabe coming for her, she knew he would come, but did he even know she had been taken by Walker? What if he thought she was with the others, either killed in the camp or taken captive by the Blackfoot. She remembered when she and Walker had started to return to the camp after their talk when the Blackfoot attacked, and they fled. At first, she thought Walker had resigned himself to not having her and letting her stay with Gabe, but when they fled, he changed.

"We have to go back! My sister!" she pleaded.

He grabbed the reins of her horse and jerked her close, hitting her across the face with a backhand and snarled, "No! You are mine now! The Blackfoot have killed them all and you will stay with me!" he demanded. He lifted his hand again as she started to protest, but she cowered under the threat.

As she remembered, she shook her head, wondering if she had forced her way if she could have escaped, but what if he was right? What if all of the camp had been killed? Would Gabe know she was not among the dead? With the lodges burned, her body could be among the dead for all he knew. She sighed heavily, dropping her chin to her chest, but a movement at the edge of the trees caught her eye and she looked first at the men, then toward the edge of the trees. There! Wolf! He was lying on his belly beneath the low hanging branches of a tall fir. She looked at him, scowling, shaking her head slightly to try to keep him back. She glanced to the men and back to the tree, but he was gone. She relaxed, looking back at the men, then glanced again at the trees, but the big wolf was no longer there. But knowing he was near, gave her hope and a touch of fear for if he came into the camp, the others would surely try to kill him.

***

Gabe stood, stretched, and walked to the horses to tighten the girths, then mounted up to start on the trail again. He was atop a rocky plateau that held several small lakes, some freshwater and fed from springs, but most were snow melt reservoirs or tanks that would dry up by late summer. As he dropped over the edge of the plateau and started down into the timbered valley, he noticed the tracks of the two horses, and more. He stepped down, looked closely at the weathered tracks and confirmed his first thoughts, Wolf! He looked at the tracks, fingered them and saw where he was following the sign of the two riders, then stood, grinning and reassured that at least Otter would not be alone.

He mounted up and took to the trail that led from the rocky plateau into the valley of a small stream that split the mountains and pushed its way to the river below. The mountains on both sides showed several slide areas where the granite peaks had shed the slab rock and pushed it into heaps that prevented any growth, save moss and lichen that clung to the slab rock, coloring the drab grey with greens and oranges. The trail Moon Walker followed was an ancient game trail that paralleled the run-off creek and danced its way through the high-country timber.

It was just past mid-day when Gabe bottomed out at the confluence of the little creek and the larger stream in the canyon bottom. Here the valley bottom spread wide and pushed the mountains away from the grassy meadows and free flowing river. This river pointed north, and the shadows of the tall ponderosa and spruce stood upon themselves as the bright sun stood alone in the blue canopy. Although the circumstances were difficult, he could not help but admire the beauty of the mountains and valley between. It was a marvelous country and seemed to be endless with mountains stacked upon mountains. He stopped at the river's edge where the stream formed a gravelly bar and stepped down, stripped the gear from the horses and grabbed a handful of pemmican for himself. He watched as the horses drank long then rolled in the dry sandy shoal then walked to the grassy bank and began to graze. He stretched out in the grass, tucked the horses leads under his back and covered his face with his hat to get a little rest himself.

After a couple hours, the sun grew warm on his chest and the horses tugged at their leads, bringing Gabe awake. With a quick glance around, he rose and brought the horses close to saddle up and start off again. The tracks followed the river downstream for about four miles before crossing the river and turning into a cut between two tall peaks. Once across the water, Gabe paused, stroking the neck of Ebony, "Well boy, I figgered that easy trail was too good to last. Looks like we gotta climb up into the tall timber again. But, from the looks of it, this won't be as bad as the last one, and there's a good stream in this 'un." He gigged the big black forward and pushed into the narrow valley, noting the tracks were deeper and fresher than before. "We're gainin' on 'em boy, yessir, we are." He looked to the sky, guessing there to be a good six to eight hours of daylight left and a clear sky, so they should make some good time. He nodded as he thought about the route, believing Moon Walker was indeed going back to his village of the *Boho'inee.* "And Shoots said that was where the three rivers met. But that's a long ways," he mused. "I hope we catch up to him long 'fore they get there!"

Gabe had called it right. The trail into the timbered valley was easier going than the rocky ascent they made the previous night to the plateau of lakes. Here the mountains sloped away with black shoulders of thick timber, and the valley bottom, although narrow, crowded against the stream but gave easy access for the trail. It was a steady climb and the air grew thin and cool. Gabe guessed that after the descent into the valley of the bigger river, and the four miles following that stream north before turning into this valley, he had already come about twelve miles. But now he came to the headwaters of the small stream and found himself in a high mountain basin, barred by a thin bald ridge that still held some snow in the crevices. He stood in his stirrups, looking at the trail that cut along the edge of the timber across the face of the ridge, then switched back to climb over a narrow saddle.

He was facing west, and the sun had dropped below the ridge, but still shone bright across the divide. He only gave it a brief thought and knew it would be better to cross in this light than later by moonlight. He gigged Ebony on and started up the trail. It was narrow and rock strewn, but the tracks of the two he pursued were evident and even the padded footprints of Wolf were obvious. They pushed on and when they faced the sheer climb, Gabe stepped down and led the way on foot, leading the horses behind. He used hands and feet to mount the ridge but was soon atop and had to step aside for the horses. He paused a moment, mounted up and rode into the trees to make a sheltered camp. The horses were winded after the climb and appreciated the rubdown after their roll. A small spring fed pool, no bigger than a hat, offered enough of a drink for both horses, but Gabe had to wait for it to refill from the slow gurgling spring. He picketed the horses, munched on some pemmican, and curled up in his blankets for some much-needed rest.

17 / Catamount

The sun had been down for no more than four hours when the snorting and pawing of Ebony brought Gabe awake. He didn't move but searched the moonlit night for whatever had the horses spooked, knowing it must be predator of some kind for the stallion to be so restless, tossing his head and sidestepping, pawing at the ground and pulling his tether tight. Whenever Gabe tethered his mount, it was with a loose tie that could be pulled free if necessary and with a toss of his head, the black was free and came to Gabe's side as he stood to his feet, rifle in hand, searching the shadows for movement. Suddenly the screaming shriek of a mountain lion split the darkness ending in a protracted growl. Ebony crowded next to Gabe, bumping him with his shoulder as the steeldust pack horse strained at its tether.

Another scream echoed across the neck of the

valley, followed by grunts and growls. Gabe turned, "That was a different one!" he said softly, as if the sound of his own voice would dispel the loneliness of the night. The first cougar spat and coughed out another screeching cry and was answered by the second. "I don't know if they're huntin' together or challenging each other, either way, we're in the middle!" muttered Gabe, reaching one hand out to stroke Ebony's neck, reassuring them both.

"That'n sounded closer," started Gabe, when the cat sprung from the trees, landing atop the steeldust and dug his claws in the mare's shoulder and buried his teeth in her neck. Gabe pulled the rifle to his shoulder and jerked off a shot, surprisingly scoring a hit on the cougar, making the beast turn to look over his shoulder at this new threat. His teeth bared and bloody, eyes shining in the moonlight, he used the back of the steeldust to launch himself at the shooter, but Gabe had pulled his pistol and cocked it as he drew, fired as the lion leaped and the bullet blossomed red in the catamount's throat. Gabe threw himself to the side and the momentum of the lion's leap carried him toward the black, but Ebony had sidestepped, and the beast fell to the ground, twitched and lay still, but Ebony had already stomped its body again and again.

Gabe searched the darkness for the second lion as he quickly reloaded the Ferguson, watching every break in the trees and shaft of moonlight for an attack.

He leaned the rifle against his hip as he reloaded the pistol then jammed it into his belt. He went to his gear and snatched up one of the saddle pistols, stuck it in his belt beside the Bailes, then picking up the rifle, he glanced to see the frizzen was down, and brought the hammer to full cock. He moved slowly, working his way to the edge of the trees that faced the clearing. Ebony stayed beside Gabe, snorting and huffing as he too searched for any danger.

Gabe couldn't help but remember the time he had his set-to in a face to face bout with another mountain lion. It had been the worst fight of his life and he had the scars to prove it, but he was also determined it would not happen again. He spun on his heels when he heard another scream and cough from behind the trees, not far away. With the rifle at his shoulder, he dropped to a crouch, scanning below the lower branches of the surrounding fir trees, when a pale streak showed in the moonlight as the second cougar lunged toward the man. The Ferguson barked and spat smoke and lead, pushing back into Gabe's shoulder, but the man did not move a step. Instantly he brought up the saddle pistol in his right hand, the belt pistol in his left and he saw the lion roll to his feet, snarl and rear back for another leap, but both pistols roared and the bullets scored as one found its mark in the neck and the other its target just below the left eye of the mountain lion. His lunge ended in a sudden drop to the ground, but he belched out a last snarl, clawing at the dirt as he breathed his last. Ebony rushed the lion, stabbing it with his front hooves and biting at its neck. Gabe had cocked the second hammer on the saddle pistol, ready to fire, but held it steady on the dead form for a moment, then stepped aside before thrusting it into his belt. He called to his black, bringing him away from the beast and to his side. He picked up his rifle, poked the body of the lion and satisfied it was dead, started reloading both the rifle and pistol. He had to take a seat on the nearby rock to steady himself and reached out to stroke the face of his big black that nuzzled him for attention.

He breathed deep, then remembered the steeldust. He rose and walked into the shadow of the trees to see the packhorse, lying on his side, twitching in pain. Gabe knelt beside the animal, examined the deep claw marks in her neck and shoulders, then the wound at the top of her neck which showed a flopping piece of flesh about the size of his hat, dangling from the mane. The wounds were too severe to survive, and he knew he had to put her down. He stroked the side of her head, spoke softly, "I'm sorry girl. You're a good one, but I can't see you suffer." He stood, drew the belt pistol and put a bullet behind her ear. The racketing echo bounced across the canyon, reminding him of his location and purpose.

He looked back at Ebony, who stood well away

from the carcasses of the lions, and walked to his friend, put his head to the stallion's and said, "Guess we might as well get a move on. Don't wanna hang around here any longer." Within moments, he had repacked the supplies and blankets, saddled the black, and they were on their way, stepping in the moonlight to make their way down the canyon's trail.

***

The big moon shone bright, slightly behind him, and followed him as he pushed into the thin timber at the top end of the valley. After just a couple miles, a tall knobby cliff rose to his left, with the shadows of the moonlight making the limestone face appear as four ogres, hollow eyes staring down on the passerby as the clatter of hooves echoed back from the stone face. Gabe's hair on the back of his neck prickled for his attention, but he slapped at his collar, and gigged Ebony to a trot. Below him, less than a mile distant, the moonlight shone bright on the white gypsum that streaked the face of a steep mountainside that had been the source of avalanches and rockslides, leaving a long slope of slide rock and rubble in its path. The rock had stacked up in the valley bottom, but time and water had pushed it aside to let the run-off past as it sought refuge in the lower climes.

The trail rose out of the canyon bottom and took to

the long shoulders of the mountain range. The mountains pushed in, but the stream and the trail found a way through. Tall timber hushed their passing, absorbing every sound and muffling every disturbance. With the only break in the monotony of silence the occasional shriek of a golden eagle that seemed to follow the travelers through the canyon.

The trail stretched through the canyon for what Gabe guessed was about ten miles since the encounter with the lions, then broke out of the timber as it joined another wider and lower valley. It had been a steady descent since they crossed the narrow ridge at the top and as he looked at the trees and other vegetation, he calculated they had dropped about six or seven thousand feet in elevation. The fir and spruce had been replaced by an occasional ponderosa, but mostly juniper and cedar and the random patches of piñon, all interspersed with the brighter green of the patches of aspen that climbed the ravines and gorges of the mountains. Alder and willow rode the banks of the river and this river was about sixty feet wide and a couple feet deep in the shallows.

Patches of green meadows dotted the valley bottom, clinging to clusters of yellow, white and blue flowers. It was a beautiful valley and one that would support vast herds of deer, elk and even moose. This was a land of plenty, but part of that plenty was plenty of Indians as well. The trail was easy and wide, made so by migrating herds and some had passed this way since Otter and Moon Walker, but their tracks showed often enough at the edges, and when Gabe recognized the tracks at the edges, he grinned, believing Otter was purposefully leaving a trail for him to follow. With the tracks of the blue roan occasionally blotted by the pads of Wolf, Gabe was also encouraged to know the black canine was still following.

Another four miles and he reined up at the mouth of the canyon, pausing before going into the flats. The rising sun had stretched the shadows long before him, and he felt the warmth at his back. He tethered Ebony in the trees and started up the slope of the mountain on the north side of the canyon. He dug his toes in, grabbed at rocks, and worked his way high up the mountainside. He spotted a shoulder with a stack of rocks in the shade of a tough piñon and bellied down with his scope in hand. He looked over the wide valley and the distant mountains as he brought the scope up and stretched it out.

As he looked, he spoke to himself, as men alone are wont to do, "I'm guessin' that big river yonder is the Yellowstone. Shoots said it was the next big river thisaway." He scanned the valley, spotted a small herd of elk close in to the mountains, a sizeable herd of antelope beyond the river in the flats, and a few deer moseying back to the trees from their early morning watering at the smaller river. He followed the Yellowstone downstream, looking at the fertile valley showing green in the morning, and saw where it cut its way through a string of foothills, making a gateway to the valley below. But when he moved the scope back to the confluence of the stream below and the Yellowstone, he spotted a thin wisp of smoke rising from the trees.

18 / Discovery

Gabe focused in on the trees at the confluence where he saw the smoke. Just before the convergence of the creek and the river, the creek bent to the left or upstream and the trees thinned into the willows. Gabe could see horses tethered in the trees, but he couldn't make out if one was the blue roan of Otter. But there were more than two. Either this was a different bunch or others had joined up with Moon Walker, either way he needed to get closer to see if Otter was there.

He searched the terrain as best he could from the distance, spotting another cut downstream, probably made by run-off or spring floods, but it had carved its way off the slight butte that bordered the river. The flat-top plateau separated the two streambeds, rising about a hundred feet above the valley floor and abruptly dropped before the riverbed of the Yellowstone. Below the confluence, the Yellowstone made a lazy bend to the west and back to the east, and Gabe judged the distance between the creek and the dry gulch to be about a mile. He thought, *That should be good cover from those in the trees, if I can make it to the cut without bein' seen.* He scoped the creek bed, drawing his sight all the way back upstream to just below his promontory. The plateau stood above the creek all the way, *If I stay well below the rise, I should make it unseen.* With one last scan, he sheathed the scope and started back down the steep slope, slipping and digging his heels all the way.

With a glance over his right shoulder at the shadowed mountains and the rising sun, he gigged Ebony around the point to take to the top of the long plateau. He looked at the wide valley before him, guessed it to be a little over five miles wide with a hedge of mountains riding the northwest edge. The bottom was fertile, showing an abundance of grasses, buffalo, Indian, gramma and more, made so by the meandering Yellowstone. The river carved its way north to push through the barrier ridge and into the great plains beyond. He moved at a walk, picking his way through the sage and greasewood clumps, dodging the yucca and cholla. As he drew nearer the river, the grasses overtook the dry land vegetation, keeping the cacti at bay.

He dropped into the draw, following its snake like twisting through the stunted piñon, until it made a straight shot toward the river. Once at the mouth of the draw, he reined up and ground tied Ebony, took the scope and mounted the butte to take a quick look toward the trees at the confluence. There was no smoke, but he could see the tethered horses and after a short scan, he crabbed back over the edge and mounted up. He neared the willows and cottonwoods at river's edge, then started downstream to be certain he was out of sight of the bunch at the trees, then searched the river for a crossing. After another mile, the river made a series of bends back on itself, but what he liked most was the opposite bank was low and just beyond it was enough of a rise that would mask his moves across the rest of the valley. His goal was to get to the valley that he guessed the bunch would take as they headed toward their village, and he wanted to try to get ahead of them. The current didn't appear too threatening, and the water was clear enough to see the gravelly bottom, but it was deep, and he knew they would be swimming.

He bent down and patted the black's neck, "Well boy, looks like we'll be goin' for a swim. So, no sense puttin' it off." He gigged the stallion off the bank and let him pick his footing as he stepped into the water. The river was about a hundred yards across and the first fifteen yards was easy going with the water not quite stirrup deep, but then Ebony dropped off an edge and they were swimming. Gabe slid from the saddle, holding onto the draw ties at the pommel and the cantle, staying downstream of the current to give Ebony freedom of movement as he turned into the current, working across the river at an angle. Within moments Gabe felt the horse reach solid footing and begin to rise from the deeper water. He pulled himself back into the saddle and they soon mounted the riverbank.

Gabe stepped down and let Ebony shake, then pulled his weapons from the scabbards and holsters and the bow and its case from beneath the fender leather. He walked to the trees and examined each one, pleased that although the case for the bow was wet on the outside, the oil treated leather had kept moisture from the bow. He was reminded of his father's admonition to always keep the bow dry, "Any water could loosen the fish glue that holds the laminate, or at the least pull the ram's horn away or even the birchbark. Always keep it dry and it'll last your lifetime!" He sat down and started working on the other weapons. As he picked up the rifle and pistols, he noted they were damp, and he sat them aside. He stood and stripped the saddle from the horse and let him roll, then returned to his weapons to reload each one. He pulled his possibles pouch around and worked almost mindlessly at the familiar tasks. And while he worked he thought of Otter. He extracted the balls and patches, cleaned the breeches and barrels, frizzens and flints and replaced the leathers that held the flints, then reloaded each one. The busy work took his mind off his mission, but never off Otter. With the holsters and scabbard in the sun, they soon dried and he replaced the weapons and mounted up.

Over the centuries the Yellowstone had pushed its way to the north, carrying with it the gravel, debris, and silt that lowered the riverbed between the wide flat plateaus that pushed against the mountains on either side. But that rise at the edge of the plateau hid the movement of long-legged black that sat beneath Gabe and stretched out across the flats with nothing more to mask their presence than the sage and greasewood abundant above and away from the river. When he scoped the valley earlier, he guessed the bunch would ride directly across the valley and take the split between the mountains that pointed to the northwest and the meeting of the three rivers.

He pointed Ebony to a cut in the mountains that would take him to the same valley and give him a chance to find a promontory where he could get a better look and hopefully locate Otter. A hogback ridge rose on his right and he followed the shoulder through the cut to a point overlooking the narrow valley. He took to the end of the hogback, tethered Ebony in the trees and climbed to the ridge, rifle and scope in hand. He would find a spot and wait, familiarizing himself with the lay of the land and maybe make some kind of plan.

He twisted around to look along the line of mountains where he lay, the upper end of the valley and
the terrain behind the mountains. Another valley
paralleled the first, framing the mountain range between them. Black timber rode the ridges and aspen
dotted the ravines and valleys. Where the creek made
its snake-like way through the basin, willows, alder,
and cottonwood shaded the banks.

He turned back to look to the south at the mouth of
the valley and watch the trail. He hunkered down to
get comfortable, thought he saw something just as he
felt the sprinkle of water on his neck. He lifted his eyes
to the black clouds that had swept overhead, letting
loose their excess baggage of water. He turned back
to look down the valley and saw four riders coming
up the trail, but they were ducking and looking for
cover. He watched as they turned into the trees on
the near side of the valley to make their way to an
overhang extending from the bluff. He had to squirm
forward, bend back to look past the timber at the edge
of the ridge, but spotted them scrambling toward the
overhang. The movement made it evident that the
one figure was a woman and Gabe was certain it was
Otter. The way she moved, her tunic and leggings, all
were familiar and even though her hands were tied,
and she was pulled along by a man, he knew it was
Otter. The other riders were tending the horses in
the trees but soon ran to the overhang to wait out

the storm. But with the overhang at their back and the clearing before them, Gabe knew he would have no access for an attack that wouldn't endanger Otter.

Gabe looked at the clouds and the rain, recognizing this wasn't just a cloudburst, but was more like a gully washer and would dump a lot of rain and the ravines and gulches would be running full, but it was also a chance for him to get well ahead of the bunch and set his ambush. He jammed the telescope back in its case and rose to walk back to the waiting Ebony, whose head was hanging and water running off his rump and neck and he was none too pleased with his place. He lifted his head as Gabe approached, shook it and stretched out his nose for his touch. Gabe chuckled, put the scope in the saddle bags and stepped up to take his wet seat.

The rain was cold and steady, but the sure-footed stallion had little difficulty as Gabe kept him on the grass and away from the trail. He crossed over the creek to let the taller mountains and shelf of the finger ridges give a little shelter from the storm that blew down from the northeast. As the rain seemed to be blowing parallel to the ground, Gabe ducked his chin into his tunic, pulled the brim of his hat over his face, and leaned into the water and wind.

He guessed the valley to be about six or seven miles long, a distance that could be covered by a good striding horse in clear weather in just over an hour, but this was different. Every step was uncertain, Ebony's head was lowered, and he leaned into the gale, occasionally slipping on the wet grass that often gave way to mud. Every ravine emptied its overflow into the valley and the usually narrow and shallow creek was now running over its banks, carrying muddy water and debris washed down from the mountainside. Gabe's sporadic glances across the narrow valley showed walls of water coming from the deeper ravines that were fed by the higher mountains anxious to shed the excess water.

It had been just over an hour and they had to ride higher up the finger ridges to keep from the overflowing creek in the bottom that now covered most of the valley floor. Once around the point of a ridge, a bowl of a basin showed, thick with timber, and beckoned to Gabe, offering a little shelter. Once in the trees, the wind was blocked but the water still came until he reached a thick cluster of towering spruce and fir with their wide spreading branches. Gabe stepped down and led Ebony into the trees. He quickly stripped the gear and rolled out his ground cover and blankets on the thick bed of spruce needles. He chopped at some of the lower branches with his hawk, wove them in among the overhead lower branches, and crawled into his blankets. The needles were dry, but the branches didn't keep out all the rain, but did shed most of it, making the makeshift shelter a warm escape. Ebony stood close in, sheltered by the long branches and the tall trees. He shook most of the water off, stomped his feet to rid more, then settled in to a welcome rest.

The smell of pine and spruce was in his nostrils as Gabe's thoughts went back to Otter, and although relieved to see her alive and moving, he was concerned about her welfare as a captive of not just one man, but three. He began thinking and calculating about how he could possibly cut the odds down. If he could separate them, he believed he would be a match for any one of them, but three at once would be a challenge, and to do it without endangering Otter. But if he could free her and even arm her, then the odds would be more in their favor. Then he thought of Wolf. Where was he? Was he still near? If so, he would be a welcome ally. And as he thought, he dozed.

19 / Ally

Ebony pawed at the still form of Gabe then dropped his nose to push against him. Gabe stirred, looked up into the flaring nostrils of Ebony and was startled awake at the sight. Ebony jerked back and the sun shone through the branches overhead. Gabe came to his feet, slapping at raindrops that slid down his neck, and looked around. The water dripped from the branches, but the sun had pushed through the storm clouds and brought with it the blue sky.

He walked into the open, looking at the valley bottom that still ran wide with floodwaters and up to the sky to see the storm clouds retreating to the southwest behind the mountains that lay along the valley's edge. The smell of fresh fallen rain, pleasant to many but stifling to Gabe, wafted across the valley carrying with it the smell of mud and debris washed down from the mountain sides. He walked to the

edge of the trees, searching the valley for any movement, but there was none other than the crashing of
floodwaters joining the overflowing creek. Yet Gabe
recognized this as an opportunity to get well ahead
of the Indians that held Otter.

Ebony was anxious to be on the move and stepped
out, picking his footing as he moved, but they stayed
well above the trees up on the shoulder above the
valley bottom. They dipped through a couple ravines
that now held but a trickle, although bits of wood and
other debris were piled at the sides. The sun was warm
on his shoulders and the valley shone green, already
the water was subsiding and the creek returning to its
banks. As he neared the head of the valley the creek
had petered out to less than two feet wide. A thicket
of willows held a small pool that was spring fed and
the trickle of water that came from the spring was the
beginning of the creek. A tall ridge on the right that
rose about seven hundred feet above the valley floor
pushed the trail to the west around a finger ridge that
came from the western mountains. Gabe reined up,
stood in his stirrups to survey the area. He twisted
back to his right where a narrow cut bent behind another finger ridge, then to his left where the sloping
ridge split and offered a brushy gulch that climbed
toward the mountain top.

The obvious choice for an ambush would be the
ridge with the cut back on the east side of the valley.

It held more timber and natural cover with several rocky outcroppings. But on the left, the narrow hogback like ridge, although with little natural cover, would have easier access and the steep slope provided ample cover for his horse. He grinned and pointed the black toward the west ridge, his eyes searching and his mind calculating. But before he rounded the narrow point, something moved from the east cut and Gabe twisted in his saddle to look.

Two furry cubs, chasing one another and wrestling when they could, came bounding from the trees. A big sow grizzly followed close behind. Probably chased from their den by the floodwaters, they were anxious to be out and about, and their mother watched while she turned over every sizable rock, looking for grubs.

Ebony smelled the threat and turned to face the mama bear and her brood. But they were three hundred plus yards away and Gabe spoke to the stallion as he bent to stroke his neck. "Easy boy, they're too far away. 'Sides, we're goin' back up thisaway." He sat up and reined the black toward the ravine and rode into the trees. The ravine proved to be a small oblong basin with a good stand of trees on the edge that faced the valley bottom and the trail below. Gabe picketed Ebony, loosened the girth, and with rifle and bow in hand, went to the tree line to watch the trail.

***

"Porcupine! You take the lead, scout ahead," ordered Moon Walker, motioning to the big man.

"Me? We do not need to scout! This is the land of our people! What danger is there?" whined the big man, stumbling toward the horses as he looked back at Moon Walker, still seated under the overhang, the woman at his side. If they were going to use the woman before killing her, he wanted to be a part, not to be sent away to scout.

"Go! Hawk will scout the back trail. If there is any one that comes for her, they will come from behind us!" growled Walker, then added, "He could have gone past in the storm and be waiting ahead. That is why you must scout!"

Although Porcupine had gained his name because he hunted and ate the quill bearing rodent, which he thought to be a delicacy, but because he also resembled the porcupine with his rotund build. His paunch hung low over the edge of his breechcloth and his leggings trailed the fringe on the ground, much like the tail of the porcupine. His temperament was also as prickly as his namesake, but he was respectful and afraid of Moon Walker and went to do his bidding.

Moon Walker turned to Red Hawk, "You scout the backtrail. But do not wait long. If he comes, and is alone, I want to be the one to kill him," he snarled as he looked toward Otter who sat with her head down. Her hands were bound, and Walker held the long strip of rawhide as he did when they were riding, always keeping her near.

"If he comes, what will you do with her?" asked Hawk, pointing with his chin.

"I will let her see me kill him, then if she does not come as my woman, I will kill her with him." He looked at Otter as he spoke, snarling with a curled lip and eyes squinted to slits. When he saw she was ignoring him, he jerked at the line, and when she glared at him, "Do you hear me woman? I will kill this white man and feed him to the coyotes! Then you will come with me!"

"I will never go with you! You are a coward, a woman killer, no woman would have you!" retorted Otter, raising her voice almost to a scream.

He jerked the line again and she fell forward, catching herself with her outstretched bound hands, only to have him kick her hands away and making her fall to her face. She rolled to the side and sat up, looked at Red Hawk, "This man you follow can only fight with women, and then only when their hands are bound!" she declared, lifting her hands for him to see the binding.

"Bah!" barked Moon Walker, jerking on the rawhide again to drag her to her feet. He motioned to Red Hawk to be on his way, and stomped toward the horses, dragging Otter behind. When Walker finished gearing up his and Otter's horses, the other warriors were gone. He lifted Otter astride the blue roan and turned to his horse, still holding the rawhide tether. But Otter grabbed a handful of mane, slapped her legs to the roan and leaned down along the mare's neck as she lunged forward. With her fingers tangled in the mane, the sudden jerk on the rawhide ripped it from Walker's hands and the roan dug deep, responding to the shouts and kicks of Otter. She burst through the trees and took to the trail, going back the way they came.

The blue roan stretched out, tail and mane flying in the wind, Otter holding to the mane and gripping with her legs, determined to make good her escape. She used her leg pressure to keep the roan on the trail, pointing the mare to the canyon where the creek had split the mountains, but first they had to cross the river. She went to the crossing they used just that morning, but the river was flowing fuller after the rain and the roan hesitated at the bank, but urged on by her rider, she splashed into the muddy water. The roan turned into the current and Otter slid from her back, keeping her hands in the mane and kicking her legs alongside. The water was frigid, and Otter felt the cold penetrating her legs, numbness began to set in as she kicked and pushed. The mare touched ground, and Otter pulled herself back aboard, exhausted. As the mare climbed the bank, her head was suddenly jerked to the side, and Otter lifted her eyes to see Red Hawk, reins gripped tightly as he pulled the mare beside the brush and reached for the woman.

Hawk dragged Otter to the ground, shoved her toward the brush as he let go the reins of the roan. He stood over the woman, a sardonic grin painting his face, "Now you will see what a real man can do for his woman!" He dropped to one knee beside her, put the other knee on her stomach and reached for the neckline of her tunic.

The blade of the tomahawk flashed in the sunlight as it descended to bury itself in the skull of the would-be assailant. Hawk let out a scream as he tried to reach for the tomahawk, but he was kicked to the side. He twisted as he fell to see Moon Walker standing over him, snarling as he growled, "She is my woman!"

Moon Walker reached for her bound wrists and jerked her to her feet. "If you try that again, I will kill you and not my warriors!" He pushed her aside and went to the horses, now standing together. He led them back to where she stood, lifted her to the back of the roan and with a tight grip on the rawhide, swung aboard his horse. He shouted and waved his hand to chase away the horse of Red Hawk and started for the river. He looked to the sun to gauge the remaining daylight, and gigged his mount into the water, followed closely by Otter.

He would go no further. He could not allow Moon Walker to keep Otter another day. For almost a week, Gabe had pursued the renegade Bannock that had taken his wife captive from the village where they were guests, and now he would bring the hunt to an end. No matter what he had to do, he was prepared. If it meant risking the life of his woman by an attack on the three warriors, it must be done for her life was at risk the longer she was in captivity. Gabe had made his resolve as he lay beneath the dark green fir trees that marched along the edge of the slope overlooking the sharp bend in the valley.

He stretched out his scope to scan the valley below, searching for any movement or sign of the approach of Otter's captors. He grinned as he watched the playful antics of the grizzly cubs, now near the edge of the creek. With the mud and silt along the banks, the cubs stayed back from the water, but the more aggressive of the two, probably a boar, repeatedly bowled the smaller one over and jumped on top. The mother glanced occasionally at her youngsters, but she was also busy at a kinnikinnick bush at creeks edge.

He moved the scope down the creek bottom, looking side to side, learning every gulch, ravine, escape route and hideaway. In any confrontation, he had been taught by his father to put himself in the position of the quarry, think like they would, see what they might see, examine their motives and work to anticipate any move they might make if there was to be a confrontation. Yet Gabe was pleased with his choice of potential battle grounds, the valley was narrow, and the only real escape was to return downstream, or try to move past this point and out of the valley to the plains beyond. Any ravine or gully that led into the valley would only offer a false out, each one ending in the face of sheer mountains. Even the low timber was sparse at best, and the valley bottom, though still wet from the rains, offered little or no cover.

He felt the air, damp and cool, was growing colder. The sun was nearing the sawtooth mountain horizon and the shadows were stretching into the valley. Dusk would come soon, but there would still be daylight enough to fight. Movement caught his attention and he adjusted the scope to see a lone rider. The big warrior of the group was walking his horse at the edge of the trail, keeping to the grass and away from the muddy path. He watched the trail before him, seldom lifting his eyes to the upper end of the valley.

Gabe followed the man with his scope as he drew near, then was surprised when the man reined his horse to the edge of the valley and into the trees at the end of the ridge opposite Gabe's position. He had a quick glimpse of the paint horse as it crested the ridge and dropped to the other side. *Maybe he's looking for a camp site, which means the others will be along shortly,* thought Gabe, then realized, *That's where that sow grizzly came from, I wonder if she's got a den back there. She sure won't like company for the night!* He moved the scope down to where the sow and cubs were, saw the big sow stand on her hind legs, watching the intruder to her territory, but when he disappeared into the draw, the sow returned to her feasting.

Although the headwater of the stream below was a short distance up the trail and just below the bend around the point, almost directly below Gabe's position, no more than a hundred fifty yards, was a small pond or backwater pool that attracted the cubs. They had waded into the shallow water and now rolled and played as if nothing else in their world mattered. The sow had come nearer but was also digging at what Gabe guessed was a strawberry or raspberry patch. She sat back on her rump and fed the berries into her

opened her eyes, looking for whoever had chased off the bear. She held her hands tight to her throat, and felt the blood running down her neck. She tried to sit up but was too weak. Then before her, Gabe went to one knee beside her, reaching for her. "Otter! Otter!" he pleaded as he lifted her to him. Wolf licked at her hand, and she smiled as darkness closed over her eyes, but she felt her man draw her close, and she was happy.

21 / Grief

He held her as her face rested on his shoulder, but she did not move. Wolf lay beside him, licking her arm and hand, whimpering, then lay still, chin resting between his paws. The western sky sent lances of gold to pierce the orange underbellies of the remaining clouds. Cool air whispered down through the pines and set the grasses in motion like waves of the sea. And still he sat, holding her, whispering to her, until the shuffling of horses' hooves through the wet grass behind him bid him turn.

"We saw Ebony, then you. Is she . . .?" asked Ezra, standing beside Grey Dove.

It took a moment for Gabe to comprehend what he saw and who was speaking. He thought maybe he was imagining this, that this was not real, a dream maybe. But when Ezra knelt beside him, he began to think more clearly, and frowned as he asked, "What, what are you doing here?" He had thought himself alone, alone with his love in his arms but not alone, she was with him. And now, so was Ezra, and Dove, and Wolf, everyone was here, and he was not alone. Things were right, as they were before, but . . . he looked down at the face of his beloved Otter. Her eyes were closed, a slight smile on her face, but she was still, so still. He looked up at Ezra, a question painting his face, then back at Otter.

Dove went to her knees on the other side, slowly reached out to touch the face of her sister and tears filled her eyes. She dropped her hand to Otter's arm, touched the blood and felt the cold and looked up at Gabe. "Did Moon Walker do this?" she asked, rocking back on her heels.

Gabe looked at her, frowned at the question, then looked back to Ezra. He looked to the face of Otter then back to Dove, "Yes," he answered simply.

Ezra nodded toward the remains of Porcupine that lay crumpled several yards away and asked, "Did Wolf do that?"

Gabe looked at Ezra, slowly turned to see the body of the warrior, and said, "Grizzly."

Ezra frowned, looked around and saw the paint horse of the Bannock grazing beyond Ebony and the blue roan of Otter. He saw the churned soil where they sat, the remnants of the panicked horses as they fought to escape the bear. In the dirt nearby was a knife, and the tether that had been a part of Otter's bonds, stretched into the grass. He stood, went to the grulla pack horse and retrieved a blanket, returned to the side of his friend and touched his shoulder. "Gabe, let's put Otter in the blanket. We need to put her to rest."

Gabe looked into the eyes of his friend, frowned, looked back at Otter and appeared to realize what had been said, then dropped his head and let tears fall on the tunic of his woman. He lifted her up for Ezra, then slid his legs from under and the two friends carefully lay her body on the blanket. Dove came close and wrapped the edges over and covered her sister, tears filling her eyes as she moved. Ezra looked at Gabe, "Where?"

Gabe frowned, trying to comprehend, then looked around. At the base of the ridge to the east, a wide patch of columbine showed purple, blue, and white, moving slowly in the evening breeze and he nodded. A cutaway in the tree line offered a camp site and as the men prepared the grave, Dove prepared the camp, gathering the firewood and starting a small cookfire. As they stood beside the grave where lay her blanket wrapped body, Gabe and Dove listened as Ezra recited from John 14:1-3 *Let not your heart be troubled: ye believe in God, believe also in me. In my Father's house are many mansions: if it were not so, I would have told you. I go to prepare a place for you. And if I go and prepare a place for you, I will come again, and receive you unto myself; that where I am, there ye may be also.* He said a simple prayer and as he finished, he lifted his eyes to his friend. Then quietly began to cover the body. Both men worked to bring rocks and stack over the grave, and when they were finished, Ezra put his arm around Gabe's shoulders and led him to the camp.

It was a quiet night, each sitting in the midst of memories and considerations, but they soon went to their blankets, Gabe off by himself, but he was soon joined by Wolf, who lay his chin on the man's chest and shared the moment of sorrow. Gabe stared at the stars, unable to make sense of his thoughts, his hand resting on Wolf's head until both drifted off to sleep.

***

Gabe's morning time in prayer was hard. He tried to pray, but his prayer turned into questions, arguments, doubts, fears, and more. But in the final moments, Gabe wept, asked forgiveness, pleaded for understanding, and shook his head in frustration as he stood to return to the camp. Dove had a good breakfast cooking and he had the first cup of coffee in well over a week. Ezra sat nearby and looked at his friend, wanting to question him, but waited for Gabe to speak when he was ready.

They ate in silence, but when the meal was over

and they sat back with coffee in hand, Gabe looked at his friend, "I'm glad you're here. But, I'm goin' after Moon Walker and it's the opposite direction from Dove's village, so . . ." he let the comment hang as a question between them and sipped on his hot java.

"I figgered you would. You wanna tell me what happened?" asked Ezra, seeing Dove stop what she was doing and sit beside her man to hear the account.

Gabe began with his description of the chase and after his third cup of coffee, finished with, "That's when you found me."

Ezra dropped his head, feeling Dove lean on his shoulder, he felt her sob as she buried her face in his tunic sleeve, and he pulled her close. The sisters had been close, more so than most, and it was only right for her to grieve, even though most of her people were more stoic than others, but she would miss not just her sister but her closest friend. Dove sighed heavily, pulled herself closer to Ezra and sat silently.

Gabe looked at his friend, "Look, I know God says vengeance is His and He will repay, and that's all well and good, but this time, His vengeance is gonna come at my hand!"

Ezra looked up, grinned, "Did you hear me argue with you on that?"

"No, but I'm lettin' you know 'fore you go preach-in' at me."

"We're goin' with you," replied Ezra, glancing at

Dove and seeing her nod.

Gabe looked at his friend for a moment, considering what he planned, then he bent down and using a stick began to draw in the dirt at their feet. "According to what Shoots said 'fore I left, Walker's people, the *Boho'inee,* do their summer hunt in the plains beyond these mountains. Somewhere, about here," he stated, pointing further northwest of their location, "is what they call the three rivers or forks that come together for the Missouri. Shoots thinks they will be camped somewhere around this area, but all of this," he motioned to his entire drawing, "is flat plains like we've seen before, good buffalo country." He sat back and looked at Ezra.

Ezra spent a few moments looking at the crude dirt map, then looked at Gabe, "You think Walker was headed there?"

"Yeah, course he didn't hang around so I could ask him, but that's what Shoots thinks too." He paused, then looked down the valley, "He did have another man with him that hasn't shown up yet."

Ezra let a slow grin paint his face, "We found him down by the big river. Had his skull split with a hawk. I recognized the tracks of Otter's blue roan nearby, and we followed those same tracks here."

"Then I reckon we might as well get a move on. Near as I can figger the three forks is a couple days or so from here and I'd like to catch up to Walker 'fore he makes it to his village. They might not like us walking into their camp and killin' one of their own."

"Prob'ly not," answered Ezra, standing and starting for the gear to pack up.

With the rising sun at their back, the three started from the low mountains, following the unmistakable tracks of the fleeing Moon Walker. As he looked at the tracks on the trail, Gabe ground his teeth, the muscles in his cheeks working and flexing, his nostrils flared and he gigged Ebony into a trot, then to a canter. Wolf matched him step for step, then ran ahead, glad to be with his people. Gabe trailed the blue roan as a pack horse. Ezra and Dove were close behind, Ezra leading the grulla pack horse and Dove riding beside him. It was good to be together again.

22 / Search

A man's mind is always active, whether awake and thinking or working, or asleep and dreaming, the mind is perpetually busy. Gabe's mind was focused on memories and emotions. The time when he first met Pale Otter, and the many times they spent together, enjoying the company of one another and getting to know one another, a friendship that grew into love and a love that became two parts of a whole when neither felt complete without the other. The steady gait of Ebony rocked him in his saddle, and he let the horse have his head as he followed the big wolf, busy trailing the fleeing Moon Walker. Everything he saw made him remember some time or happening with Otter, the flowers reminded him of her love for the blossoms of spring, the tall ponderosa with it long needles of their times together in the woods, the blue sky of her smile and joy that always showed in her eyes.

He sighed heavily, looking around to focus on the present. They came from a wide basin and draw that bent into a narrow valley bordered by timbered and rocky slopes of mountain ridges. The trail pointed due west and the mountains stepped back to show the vast plains in the distance. But even the view of the far-ranging lands reminded him of her, and a glance at a rock formation on the south side of the narrows, took him back to the time he and Ezra had shared with the sisters from the Bible. Otter was the more curious of the two and had started them on the discussion of the Christian beliefs and Heaven. When they opened the Bible and started showing the verses that explained the way of salvation, she had leaned forward, totally focused on every word, and when Gabe said, "There's four things we each need to know," and began explaining how those four things were that everyone was a sinner, that sin had a penalty of death and hell forever, but that Christ paid that penalty for us and purchased the gift of eternal life for anyone and everyone that would believe. Otter smiled and clapped her hands and leaned forward and asked, "How can I get that gift?"

Gabe chuckled at the memory and pictured the sisters both bowing their heads and praying, asking God for that gift and forgiveness of their sins. They both ended their prayer in thanks to God for that amazing gift of eternal life and knowing they would one day spend their eternity in Heaven with Him. Gabe dropped his head, feeling as if he had been struck in his chest as the pain of losing his love almost bent him over. But as he breathed deep, he lifted up and looked to the sky and asked, "Why? Why did you have to take her?"

"He didn't take her, but He received her!" Gabe was startled at the words, shook his head and looked around to see Ezra riding beside him, arms crossed as he leaned forward on the pommel of his saddle. "Just be glad you know she's in Heaven and someday you'll see her again."

Gabe stared at him, "I must have said that out loud," as he looked sideways at his friend.

"Ummhmm, you did."

"Good, cuz when you answered it scared me! I thought it was God!"

Ezra chuckled, shaking his head, "Well that's a first. I ain't never been mistook for God!"

Gabe looked ahead as the narrow valley opened to the plains, then pointed to the trees at the edge of the creek, "Look's like a good place to stop and stretch, give the horses a breather."

Ezra nodded, turned to motion to Grey Dove, and they went to the trees. They had traveled about ten miles, but with the late start, they were making good progress. The sun was high in the cloudless sky and the warmth penetrated their buckskins, making them seek the shade of the few cottonwoods that rose from the thicker willows and other brush. It would be a short stop, just long enough for a cup of chicory/coffee and some pemmican and a johnnycake or two. The horses already had their noses in the tall grass and Dove had the coffee pot bouncing on the hot coals. Gabe took to the stack of rocks for his usual scan of the trail ahead, Wolf at his side.

"Saw a bunch of buffalo, but they're a long ways out there. Some antelope, a deer, a coyote, but nothin' else. But that land's just like what we've seen before, where you think there's nothin' there could be a whole village or a war party or more. That rollin' land is like that," declared Gabe as he accepted the coffee from Dove.

"Could be worse. At least with the rain yesterday, we won't be chokin' on our own dust," responded Ezra, sipping on his black brew.

"Yeah, but I didn't see any water either. We might have a dry camp tonite."

"Then we better make sure we got water. I can do without most anything, but I get kinda cranky when I don't have my coffee," grumbled Ezra, chuckling.

"Ain't that the truth! But what's your excuse for other times?"

Ezra frowned, "Other times? Ain't no other times that I'm cranky. I'll have you know I'm the most even-tempered friend you have!"

"Ezra, you're the only friend I have!" countered Gabe, laughing at his friend.

"Oh. Well, see there. I was right, wasn't I?"

Gabe chuckled, stood and tossed the dregs of his coffee to the bushes and started for his horse. Over his shoulder he said, "Alright my only friend, let's hit the leather and make some time!" He pulled on the pommel to settle the saddle in place, tightened the girth, and started to swing aboard when a soft voice at his elbow stopped him, "Am I not your friend also?"

Gabe turned back to look at the big eyes of Grey Dove, "You are more than a friend, you are my sister, my friend's wife, and our companion. Yes, Dove, you are a friend." He enveloped her in his arms and drew her close for a hug of friendship and shared sorrow. They held that for just a moment, then Gabe pulled back, looked in her eyes, and said, "Don't ever forget that. We are family."

She dabbed at a tear, forced a smile and nodded. As she stepped back, Gabe stepped aboard Ebony and watched as Dove went to her horse. Ezra had readied both mounts and stood beside her buckskin, gave her a hand up and went to his bay and stepped into the saddle. With a hand motion, Wolf took off on the trail and Gabe pointed Ebony after, trailing the blue roan behind.

But there was water, a trickle of a creek led the way from the canyon and soon joined another, that followed the long line of rolling foothills that marched beside them on the north edge of the wide basin. Yet it was dryer land, yucca, prickly bear, cholla, sage, greasewood and rabbit brush grew in abundance. But most of the flat land showed buffalo grass and the blue shades of gramma. And the trail of the fleeing Bannock showed plainly in the soil made moist by the rain.

Gabe often stood in his stirrups to stretch his legs and to look around at the land that few if any white men had seen. Although when he was at university, he had studied all he could about the land known as New Spain since before he was born, it was still a mostly unexplored land. He had read Bourgmont's *The Route to be Taken to Ascend the Missouri River* and had seen the map of Guillaume Delisle that showed much of the land west of the Mississippi, this land before him had seen little of the Spanish or the French before them. This was land known by the Shoshone, Bannock, Blackfoot, and Salish, but not by those that were not native to this land. He had read about French traders and the Hudson Bay Company and their attempts to explore and trade in the land of the upper Missouri, and even the more recent expedition of Jacques D'Eglise, but none had told of this land that lay before them now.

He recalled the men that were a part of the expedition of the Company of Discoverers and Explorers of the Missouri that had tried to earn the reward offered for the first person to reach the Pacific Ocean via the Missouri river, and how they had failed. But those same men had told about the Kootenai, the Blackfoot, and the Salish peoples, and had spent the winter with the Kootenai. But none had come to the three rivers that fed the Missouri. Perhaps they would be the first.

A dip in the foothills to the right caught Gabe's attention and he reined up to look through the cut. Tall granite peaks seemed to march in formation off to the north, spreading their cloaks of timber down the slopes and into the valley's edge. He looked back to the west where the plains stretched out to be bordered by other mountains, not so high as the others, but enough to make a sawtooth horizon that caught the pale blue of distant sky and held it as though cradling the very edge of eternity.

To the south, more mountains stood together, some reaching well over ten thousand feet, not so high as those they crossed in the Absaroka Range, but granite tipped peaks that still clutched small patches of glacier ice and snow. These were the mountains that would one day bear the name of the Gallatin Range, but now were just known as the mountains beyond the plains. They held to the edge of the foothills on the north end of the plains, yet the setting sun was almost blinding as they headed due west. Gabe chose to stop at the first draw that offered water. It was a small creek that was probably dry most of the year, but still held run-off from the previous day's rain. A low butte offered cover and with a cluster of stunted cottonwoods and thick alders, interspersed with chokecherry bushes, at the edge of the creek, they opted to make camp.

23 / Visitor

It was a restless night for Gabe, his mind chasing memories and the reality of the images in his dreams were troublesome. He drifted off sometime after midnight, but a low growl from Wolf who lay at his side, brought him instantly awake. Unmoving, he scanned the camp, first to the horses who showed no alarm, then to the sleeping forms of Ezra and Dove. Almost a whisper, the low growl came again. A quick glance at Wolf then to where he looked, and Gabe saw a form sitting near the coals of the fire. A man, white hair showing in the moonlight, hunkered on the log, hands stretched toward the glowing embers. He was Indian, his thin frame held sagging buckskins, but he did not move.

A whisper came from the darkness, "I seek only warmth, I will do no harm."

Gabe slowly rolled from his blankets, stood and

walked toward the man. He sat on a rock opposite, picked up a couple sticks and lay them on the coals. Soon hungry flames licked at the fresh wood, and in the flare, Gabe saw a weathered old man, wrinkled and somber face, sadness in his eyes that stared at the flames.

Gabe spoke in Shoshone, "Are you hungry?" making signs as he asked the question.

The old man looked up at him, nodded, and dropped his eyes to the flames. Gabe went to the parfleche, got a handful of pemmican, a johnny cake, and the coffee pot. He handed the food to the old man, who nodded and started eating right away. When Gabe returned with the coffee pot full of water, he dropped a handful of chicory and coffee in, then sat it by the fire and returned to his seat. When the old man had finished off the bit of food, Gabe asked, "Where are your people?"

The old man looked up at him and started, "I am Lone Eagle of the *Doyahinee* or the Mountain People of the *Tukkutikka* band of the Shoshone. My people were on our buffalo hunt with the *Agaidika* in the time *daza mea',* when my wife became ill. The daughter of my daughter, Little Squirrel, stayed with us to tend to her grandmother. We were camped in the next draw," he nodded to the bluff to the west. "Then came a man, the war leader of the *Boho'inee.* We fed him, then he wanted Little Squirrel, said he would take her as his woman. But I could not give her, that is for her father to do. But he wanted her, and we fought, then he killed my woman, and when Little Squirrel kicked him where it hurts, he cut her throat."

"He killed your woman and the girl?" asked Gabe.

"Yes," replied the old man. It was then that Gabe noticed how Lone Eagle held himself, with his forearm across his stomach.

"You are hurt," added Gabe, standing to go to the man's side. Ezra and Dove had awakened as the man talked and now came closer, Dove stepping beside the man and gently pulling at his arm to look at the wounds. She spoke to Ezra, "Bring a blanket."

The men steadied the old man as they lay him on the blanket for Dove to tend his wounds. When she pulled back the tunic, they saw two knife deep knife wounds, one torn to the side. Lone Eagle looked at Dove, "I will soon cross over with my woman." He looked up at Gabe, "My woman and the girl must be buried."

"We'll take care of it, Lone Eagle. You let this woman tend your wounds, Black Buffalo and I will go to your lodge and see to those who have already crossed over."

"It is good," answered Lone Eagle, then turned his head to the side, let out a long sigh and breathed his last.

Gabe looked at Ezra, "Did you hear what he said about what happened?"

"Just that someone killed his woman," answered Ezra.

"Moon Walker tried to take the old man's grand-daughter, but Lone Eagle fought him as did his woman. Walker probably thought he'd killed the old man, so he killed the woman and was gonna take the girl, but she gave him a well-placed kick that caused Walker to cut her throat."

Ezra dropped his eyes, shaking his head, and looked at the old man. He bent to his side and started wrapping the body in the blanket, and with a nod to Gabe, the two men carried his body to the edge of the camp near the horses. Ezra looked to the horses, then over his shoulder he added, "Since we're all up and about, might as well have somethin' to eat and get on the trail. We'll need to stop and take care of the old man's family."

"Ummhmm," answered Gabe, pulling the dancing coffee pot back from the flames.

***

Three graves lay side by side at the edge of the bluff, a cluster of juniper cast their shade over the rocks that covered the mounds and the trail of a travois led away from the site. The personal belongings of Lone Eagle and his family that were not buried with them, were rolled up in the hide cover of the tipi that rode on the travois. The old man had apparently bagged a couple buffalo and the woman had been working the hides that were bundled with the tipi. It was a somber group that rode from the gravesite, the rising sun at their backs.

A lot can be told about a man by the trail he leaves. The tracks of the horse told the story of a man that had no respect nor concern for the animal that bore him. Although the tracks pointed due west, whenever he came to a pile of rocks, cactus, or any other obstacle, he forced the animal to go through, never around. Although they needed no confirmation of the lack of character of the man they followed, a man that killed innocent women and others with no remorse, when there was no need other than to satisfy his blood lust, and showed no concern for the horse that carried him, was a man that had no conscience nor worth in this world.

Gabe sighed heavily as he followed the tracks, knowing that with every step they were drawing closer to the confrontation he wanted. The image of Moon Walker's knife slashing at the throat of Otter caused the anger to boil within his chest and the bile to rise in his throat. He shook his head as he remembered the many passages of scripture that spoke of vengeance belonging to God, and he muttered, "Just let me be the weapon you use to bring vengeance upon that man. The longer he lives, the more lives he destroys!"

"What? What'd you say?" asked Ezra from behind.

"Nothin'!, just nothin'!" growled Gabe.

Ezra looked at Dove and spoke softly, "He's mad-der'n I ever seen him. If we catch up to Moon Walker, it ain't gonna be fun to watch!"

"Moon Walker is known as a great warrior. No one has beat him in battle. Gabe must be aware and careful, Walker is brutal," responded Dove.

"I've seen Gabe really angry one time, and the man was bigger'n Moon Walker and a fighter, but when Gabe tore into him, it didn't last long a'tall. And I know of one other time, that was when a high and mighty cock o'the walk insulted his sister. It took four men to keep him back, and the next day, Gabe killed him in a duel. So, our friend can handle himself, and with his anger up like it is . . ." he let the thought dangle between them as they both considered what lay before them.

They followed the edge of the long plateaus and buttes that marked the dry land to the north, with the winding river that would one day be known as the Gallatin on their left. But when the river pushed against the buttes, the tracks of Moon Walker crossed over to the grassy flatlands but continued westerly. It was approaching mid-day when a line of flattops pushed from the southwest toward the river they followed, crowding it in to the buttes on their right. Beyond the point, another part of the vast plains opened to show the greenery that held the other two forks that rushed toward the confluence with the Missouri. But what caught their attention was the conglomeration of tipis, brush huts, and lean-to shelters that made up the village of the *Agai·ika* and the *Boho'inee*, Moon Walker's people.

When they looked at Walker's tracks, it was evident he had kicked his mount into a gallop as he rushed to cross the river and join his village. Gabe looked at Ezra, "Whaddya think?"

Ezra stood in his stirrups staring beyond the village at the point where the rivers converged. He nodded, then pointed, "What's that?"

Gabe stood, looking where Ezra pointed, then dropped into his seat and twisted around to retrieve his brass telescope. He cocked his leg around to rest on his pommel, used it for a rest, and lifted the scope to look. As he scanned the area, he spoke softly, "Well, I'll be a monkey's uncle!"

"What is it?" asked Ezra, watching Gabe as he turned to hand the scope to his friend.

"Take a look-see."

"Is that?" started Ezra, then dropped the scope to look at Gabe.

"Ummhmm, that's a wall tent. Must be some traders."

24 / Traders

It was a fertile valley, trees, shrubs, brush, grasses all grew in abundance. Along the waterways cottonwoods towered over a hundred feet tall. Alder, ash, chokecherry, and maple grew as small trees or brush where it was crowded. A variety of pine and fir mingled with aspen on the peninsulas and islands and climbing up the slopes of the nearby mountains, until the juniper crowded in from the dryer hills. The village was nestled between the winding river and the rimrock buttes on the north edge of the vast flatlands.

The river followed by Gabe and company would one day be known as the Gallatin, and the other two forks would be named the Madison and the Jefferson, but now they were just known as the three forks of the headwaters of the Missouri. All three were mature streams that twisted their way through the plains like snakes on a hot rock, until forced together to exit to the north and vast faraway lands.

The wall tents spotted by Gabe were between the Gallatin and the tall buttes that marked the confluence of the rivers, and downstream about a mile from the village of the *Agaidika* and the *Boho'inee.* As Gabe slid the scope into the case and into his saddlebags, Dove came closer and asked, "What are you going to do?"

"I'm thinkin' on it Dove. I'm not sure."

She paused, looked from Ezra back to Gabe, and asked, "Perhaps it would be best for me to go into the village, meet the people and see what Moon Walker is doing."

Gabe frowned, "But why? And it might not be safe for you."

Ezra gigged his bay horse closer and listened, then added, "She's Shoshone and knows some of those people."

"But if Moon Walker saw her, no tellin' what he'd do!" responded Gabe, concerned.

"He could do nothing! I am Shoshone!" She spat the words, contempt and anger showing in her eyes. "These are Shoshone! He is Bannock! These people took him in because of his mother, and he became a war leader because of his cruelty. But they know what he is, and I will tell them *who* he is and what he has done!"

Gabe looked at her, then to the ground and sighed heavily. "Dove, there's nothing I would like better than to go charging in there and take that man down.

But we will not risk you to do it! But," he paused as he looked from Dove to Ezra, "If Ezra agrees, then maybe you can go in there, as long as you give us your word you will not confront Moon Walker or talk to anybody about him, except to find out about him. Don't go sticking the hornet's nest until we come into the village."

"You will come?" asked Dove, looking from Gabe to Ezra.

"Ummhmm, we're gonna go see these traders and see what they're up to, maybe pitch camp nearby. You can talk about Lone Eagle and his family, find out about Little Squirrel's mother, and just find out where Moon Walker is and what he's doin', but that's all!" He ducked his head and glared at her from under his dark brows, waiting for an answer. He glanced at Ezra, saw him nod, and then to Dove.

"I will do as you say," she answered, quietly.

"Then come down to the point yonder where the traders are, we'll pitch camp near there. 'Sides, you know more about gettin' that tipi up than we do anyway," he grinned.

She laughed and reined her buckskin around, pointing the gelding to the river to cross over to the village. She turned back to wave at Ezra, and the men started toward the Trader's camp. They were shielded from sight by the villagers with the tall cottonwoods that grew along the bank of the Gallatin and soon were almost a mile downriver from the village. Before them thick stands of cattails and stunted willows told of boggy land and the river forked and forked again to spread across the flats. With other dry river beds where the waters had flowed before and would again when spring runoff came, and smaller feeder streams, it seemed the area was as much water as grassland. The men chose to cross over, wading the shallow waters that only came to the horses knees, then across another fork of a stream, before rising to higher grassland that lay in the shadow of the buttes that marked the northern limits of the vast park area.

As they neared the camp of two wall tents, they were hailed and greeted by two men that were busy with stacks of pelts. "Step down! Step down! I am surprised to see other traders here! I was certain we were the first!"

Gabe chuckled, "Oh, you're the first alright. We're not traders, just well," he glanced at Ezra, "I guess you could say we're just wanderers." He stepped forward and extended his hand to shake, "I'm Gabe Stone, and this is my friend, Ezra Blackwell."

As Ezra stepped forward, both traders extended their hands as the first man spoke again. "And I am Alexander Henry, and this is my friend and companion, David Thompson." As the men shook hands, Henry said, "So, wanderers huh? Been in the mountains long?"

"Quite a spell, but not near long enough," answered

Gabe, chuckling and scratching at his cheek whiskers as he spoke. "This country kinda gets in your blood, if you know what I mean."

"I do indeed. We've been exploring for quite a spell ourselves. Covered much of Canada and the north country, now we're bound for the Pacific."

Gabe raised his eyebrows, "Alexander Henry, of the North West Company?" he frowned a little skeptically.

Henry grinned, "No, that would be my uncle of the same name. I'm not quite that old yet. But I was a partner with the company, and the Pacific Fur Company as well. Now that we've come to the headwaters of the Missouri, we know this won't take us to the Pacific, so . . ."

Gabe looked at the wall tents and the stacks of gear, then asked, "Tradin' with the Indians are you?"

"A little. But we don't want to get too loaded down with pelts and such, so, we're just tradin' mostly for foodstuffs, you know, pemmican, smoked meat and vegetables like turnips, timpsila, camas, that sort."

"Been here long?" asked Ezra.

"Just a couple days. The village was here, had a hunt for buffalo, south a bit, did well too. They've been friendly enough."

Gabe lifted his head slowly, considering the men and his plans. "Then you won't mind if we camp nearby?"

"Glad to have you. The rest of our men are down-river in the canyon, looking for meat, but they'll be back soon. You're welcome to come back and meet the others, if you're of a mind to, we've got coffee."

Ezra perked up at the mention of coffee, "Got enough to trade?"

Henry grinned, "We might part with a little. What'chu got?"

"Oh, couple fresh buffalo hides, might find sumpin' else."

"We'll talk when you all come back later," replied Henry.

They picked a spot near the river, tall cottonwoods and some maples offering ample shade and windbreak, and dropped the travois, stripped the gear from the horses and rubbed them down after they had a roll in the grass. It took both men to wrestle the hide tipi off the travois and spread it out. Once the first tripod of poles was standing, they lay the other lodgepole pine poles into the cradle and spaced them out, tossed the rope over the peak and started to pull the tipi up the poles. Dove had arrived, unseen, and watched the men struggle to erect the lodge, snickering to herself as she stood in the trees observing their labors. When the hide was pulled to the top, they began stretching it around the frame, and Dove came to their rescue to guide them as the placed the door facing the east, adjusted the smoke flaps, and bound the pieces together with the stick lacing.

While Gabe put their gear inside and lay out the

blankets and robes, Ezra gathered the firewood and got the fire going, allowing Dove to prepare the meal of broiled venison strip steaks, roasted turnips and camas, and some boiled fresh greens. Once they finished, Dove began telling of her discoveries in the village. "Moon Walker blamed the deaths of Porcupine and Red Hawk, his two warriors, on the attack of the Blackfoot. He told of his bravery in the attack and how he rescued several women who returned to their village. He also told of two men, non-natives, that had helped the Blackfoot and were following him."

"He must have been talking about us," suggested Ezra.

Gabe and Dove both nodded, then Dove added, "I spoke to Lone Eagle's daughter. She will tell of Moon Walker after we come into the village."

"Who's the chief?"

"Holder of Badgers is the chief. Two Moons is the shaman."

"Will he allow us to confront Moon Walker, make him pay?" asked Gabe.

"Because you are a friend to the Shoshone and your woman was a Shoshone, you have that right. He will not stop you, and when he hears what Moon Walker has done, he will prevent Moon Walker from leaving," answered Dove. "But if Moon Walker kills you, they will say your medicine was bad and Walker will be even more honored."

"What if I choose to fight him?" asked Ezra.

"After?"

"Yes."

"You will have that right, because he," nodding toward Gabe, "is your brother."

The men looked at one another, nodded, and sat silent, thinking about tomorrow.

25 / Council

Dove led the way as the three rode into the village of the *Agai·ika* and the *Boho'inee.* Word quickly spread and went before them, several coming close to look at the intruders. Although many carried on with their daily routines, paying little attention to the visitors. Women were busy working at hides, on their knees, scraping and stretching, others busy at cook fires, tending stews and other foodstuffs, and still others were busy with handcrafts, making buckskins, beading moccasins, and more. Children were playing some hoop game, others practicing with small bows and dull arrows, while older youngsters were tending the horses at the herd grazing near the river.

But several warriors, some carrying lances, others with bows in hand but without arrows nocked, some with hands on knives or tomahawks in their belts, casually followed the three riders toward the center of the village. Gabe sat tall aboard the high-stepping Ebony. The sheen of the stallion's coat showing bright in the morning sun, his long legs lifted, and his head was raised, his neck arched as he seemed to enjoy the attention of the horde. Gabe's long dark blonde hair dangled over his collar, his sun-bleached whiskers contrasted with his dark-tanned skin. Yet the image of the big black wolf that trotted beside the black stallion made many catch their breath and step back, putting their hands to the children to keep them in check. But the attention of the throng quickly turned to the dark man. Shoulders as broad, and chest as deep as a charging buffalo only enhanced the thoughts of those that saw this buffalo man who sat proudly atop the well-muscled bay gelding. Word spread by shouted announcements and warnings and people came from their mundane duties to see what was so alarming.

Two lance holding warriors stepped before them as Dove and the men quickly reined up. The warriors took hold of the bridles of the horses and motioned for the three to step down. Gabe glanced beyond the two men to see who he suspected was the chief and his shaman standing before the big lodge, watching their arrival, while another man, Moon Walker, stood nearby.

When they stood before the two warriors, Gabe addressed them in the Shoshone tongue, "I am Spirit Bear, this," nodding to Ezra, "is Black Buffalo and his woman, Grey Dove, of the *Kuccuntikka* Shoshone.

We seek a council with Holder of Badgers and his Shaman, Two Moons."

One of the two guards turned on his heel and went to the men standing before the big lodge, apparently reporting on what was said, then quickly returned to escort the three before the chief. The chief stood with a thin blanket over one shoulder, a brawny shoulder and silver-banded arm exposed. His broad shoulders and stance spoke of confidence and strength, while his eyes showed both curiosity and skepticism. Three notched feathers dangled from a scalp-lock at the back of his head and a beaded necklace hung at his throat. The shaman stood at the chief's left side, a blanket covering both shoulders, but a necklace of beads and totem bags and a headband with two buffalo horns told of his rank.

The chief breathed deep, lifting his shoulders and flexing his chest muscles, his nostrils flared, and a scorn tripped the edge of his lip. He lifted his head, glanced at the wolf, then looked down his nose at Gabe, even though Gabe was half a hand taller, and asked, "Why do you enter our village?" It was both a demand and a threat, as his eyes flashed from Gabe to Ezra.

"I am Spirit Bear, and this is Black Buffalo and his woman, Grey Dove, of the *Kuccuntikka* Shoshone. We come to seek a council with the great Holder of Badgers, the chief of the *Agaidika*."

"Why should we have a council for you?" spat the

chief, indignant with this white man that dared to enter their village uninvited. Moon Walker, their own war leader, had already spoken of these men as enemies of the Shoshone.

"My wife was the sister of Grey Dove and as her husband I have the right to ask for a council with you and your shaman, because her death was at the hand of one of your people." Dove stepped closer as did Ezra, as they waited for the chief's response. The custom of his people required him to give this man a council, but he was hesitant after the report given by Moon Walker. The chief paused, dropped his eyes, then turned to a small group that stood slightly behind him and to his right. Three men, undoubtedly elders as evidenced by their position near the chief and the grey highlights in their hair as well as their obvious stance as warriors and leaders. The men conferred for just a moment, and as the chief turned back to Gabe the elders walked behind him and into the lodge.

"We will talk," answered the chief, and abruptly turned his back on Gabe and followed his shaman into the lodge. Moon Walker had joined another warrior and stepped before Gabe to follow the chief into the lodge. Dove looked at Gabe, "You will be seated across the fire from the chief, facing him. Ezra will be on your right and I will be beside him. Moon Walker is a war leader and will be seated behind the chief and the shaman and the elders. You can only speak when the chief allows it."

Gabe nodded and with a glance to Ezra, let Dove and his friend preceded him into the lodge. He ducked through the entry, stood upright as soon as he could and looked around the dim interior. Although the sunlight came from the smoke hole and illuminated the sidewalls, most of the interior was in a shadow. He noted a few others, some women, gathered at the back of the lodge, and with a glance at the chief who motioned him to be seated before him, took the proffered place and sat with legs crossed before him.

The handle of his tomahawk pushed from the ground and the metal head poked him in the ribs causing him to adjust it for comfort. Then he adjusted the pistol in his belt, relaxed and pushed his shoulders back as he arched his back, then settled down to look at those before him. To the left of the chief sat the shaman, Two Moons, and to his right, the three elders, all sitting somber faced and staring at Gabe and company. Gabe could tell by the stares and mumbled comments, many had never seen a black man like Ezra, and some were confounded or confused at this man named Black Buffalo that sat before them. Gabe let a little grin cross his face as he spoke softly to Ezra, "I think Black Buffalo has some of them a little baffled."

Ezra grinned, "Just wait till I let out a beller like a big bull!"

Gabe shook his head and dropped his eyes to put a somber expression on his face before looking back to the chief. The chief accepted a pipe from a nearby elder, lit it with a brand from the small fire before them, then lifted the pipe to the four directions, above his head to the heavens and before him to the earth, the took a long draw, exhaled, and offered the pipe to the nearest elder. The motions were repeated by each man, and the last elder handed the pipe to Gabe. He too, lifted the pipe as did the others, then after taking a long draw and exhaling, passed the pipe to Ezra. He did the same, then passed it to the shaman, who was the last to repeat the action, then sat the pipe aside. The shaman nodded to the chief and Holder of Badgers spoke, "You have your council. Say what you must."

Gabe breathed deep, then lifted his eyes to the chief, "Several summers ago when the Shoshone assembled for the grand encampment, I was told that Moon Walker," he nodded toward the war leader, "asked the father of Grey Dove for the first born daughter of Red Pipe. The leader of the *Kuccuntikka* would not give his daughter to Moon Walker. But at the end of the next summer, Red Pipe agreed to allow his daughter to become my wife, and to have Grey Dove become the wife of Black Buffalo. We met Moon Walker when we visited the village of Owitze and he tried then to take my woman, but she would have nothing to do with him. But later, when we were with Shoots Running Buffalo on a hunt, the Blackfoot attacked the camp while we were gone to scout the buffalo herd. The

Blackfoot took all the women and children that were left alive as captives. But Moon Walker had taken my woman before the Blackfoot attacked."

The mention of an attack by the Blackfoot stirred most of those, all showing anger and leaned forward to hear more. The chief looked unmoved, for he had heard of this from Moon Walker just the day before. Gabe noted his lack of response, and suspected something, but continued with his story.

"Shoots Running Buffalo and all of the warriors went after the Blackfoot, caught them and killed most of them and took the women back." At this word of a victory, the men all shouted and beat their fists on the ground, talking to one another, but soon stilled and looked at Gabe. The chief asked, "Did you go with Shoots Running Buffalo?"

"I scouted before the others. Black Buffalo," he nodded toward Ezra, "came with Shoots and the others. I attacked from the mouth of the canyon, Shoots and the others from behind."

The chief slowly nodded his head, "How many Blackfoot were killed?"

Gabe looked at Ezra, then back at the chief, "All but two who ran away. There were about three hands of dead Blackfoot."

"How many Shoshone were killed?"

"Only the old ones and other women and children at the camp. None at the battle."

The chief nodded, looked at the elders and the shaman, then back to Gabe, but frowned and turned to Grey Dove. "Were you a captive of the Blackfoot?"

"Yes."

"Did you see this battle?"

"Yes."

"Was the battle as he says?"

At the implication of a lie, Gabe's chest swelled, and his eyes glared, but he held himself in check to await the answer of Dove.

"Yes, but ..." started Dove, then looked from Ezra to Gabe.

"But what?" asked the chief, expecting something that would condemn the white man and give truth to what Moon Walker had reported. He held up his hand before she answered, and asked, "Was Moon Walker at this battle?"

Dove glared at the chief and then at Moon Walker, she looked back at the chief, and spat, "NO! He had taken my sister and ran away!"

The elders looked at one another, some turning to look back at their war leader, then to the chief, who spoke again, "You were asked if the battle was as he said."

Dove nodded and began her account of what she saw as Gabe fought the Blackfoot. "This man was alone and stopped the entire war party by himself. He was above the meadow and took several with his bow from a great distance. As they tried to get to him, he killed others with his rifle and pistols. Shoots Running Buffalo believed this man killed almost two hands of Blackfoot!" She motioned to her man, "And Black Buffalo used his war club and killed this many," she added as she held up four fingers.

The chief looked at the others, then back at Gabe, and said, "After the battle, what did you do?"

"I found out from Grey Dove that Moon Walker had taken my woman. I went back to the camp to find his trail and follow him. I traveled for two hands of days when I found him. But when a sow grizzly attacked the man known as Porcupine to defend her cubs and then turned on Moon Walker, that coward attacked my woman. Her hands were tied, and he had a rawhide tether on her throat, and he cut her throat to throw her in front of the grizzly so he could escape!" Gabe had snarled the last words, biting each one off as he glared at the war leader sitting behind the others.

Moon Walker jumped to his feet, shaking his fist toward Gabe and shouted, "He lies! This white man, like all others, lies! You cannot believe what he says! I am Moon Walker; I am your war leader!" He stood, arms held stiffly at his sides as he leaned into his words, thinking his shouted words would be accepted as the truth, even though he knew he was the liar.

Holds the Badgers snarled at the man, "Quiet! Sit!"

Moon Walker glared at the chief, but sat down, folding his arms across his chest and staring at Gabe.

Dove asked, "May I say more?"

The chief nodded.

"After he killed my sister, we followed him. When we were at camp, the father of Yellow Bird of your people, came into our camp. He told us that this man, Moon Walker, had come into his camp, ate of his food, then tried to take the daughter of Yellow Bird for his woman. Her grandfather refused, and Moon Walker stabbed him, killed his woman, tried to take the girl, but she resisted by kicking him in his man place. Moon Walker was angered and killed her, then he stole from the dead and left. The old man told us of this before he crossed over. We buried him and his woman and his granddaughter, but first promised to tell you about this man's wrongdoing."

As Dove leaned back, the chief dropped his eyes as he sighed heavily. He wanted to believe his war leader, but he knew the man and knew his way with women. What he had heard was true to way of the man, and he had to believe this woman of the Shoshone and the two men who were accepted as part of another band of the Shoshone. He looked at the elders, who sat stoically, anger flaring in their eyes. He looked at the shaman and saw the same response. For Moon Walker had killed of his own people and taken the life of an old and respected leader of the people and his woman and his young granddaughter. These were terrible things and worthy of death or banishment.

Holder of Badgers looked at Gabe and asked, "What is it you ask?"

"I ask for my right to honor the blood of my woman and my friend, the father of Yellow Bird and take the blood of their killer." He had been careful to not use the names of the departed, as was the way of the people, but he so wanted to shout Pale Otter to the others, so her name would be remembered, but he restrained himself.

"Moon Walker is a war leader of our people because he is known as a fierce fighter and great warrior. If he defeats you, he will kill you. Do you still want to face him?"

Gabe couldn't help but chuckle at the chief's words, for he had no doubt it would be a fight to the finish, but he was determined to exact what he thought of as the vengeance of the Lord against this despicable murderer. "Yes, I will not only face him, I will spill his blood in the dirt where it belongs."

26 / Vengeance

Gabe slipped the claw necklace over his head, handing it to Dove as he and Ezra looked at the assembling warriors. The council had agreed to the vengeance battle, the chief and elders in agreement with the purpose and the need. Moon Walker had won his position as war leader based solely on his prowess in battle, but the elders had known he was less than expected for a leader of men.

Most warriors were eager to follow a proven warrior into any conflict, not just because he was a good warrior, but because he could lead his men to victory, whether as a war party or on a raid for captives, booty, and honors. But Walker had shown himself to be less of a leader and more of a warrior solely concerned about his own honors and conquests, always choosing whatever position or opponent assured his triumph, letting his followers take what was left. As a result, he found few warriors that would willingly follow him into battle.

And when they heard of his murderous rampage, most had turned against him. Yet even in those instances, there always seems to be followers that will see what they want to see and cast aside any doubts or accusations. And Moon Walker had a faithful following that believed the accusations were false or that Walker had his reasons, and they found it easier to stand behind him rather than accept a white man and his challenge.

As the warriors began to form a large circle, Yellow Bird walked to the side of Grey Dove, nodded, then looked at Gabe, "This," motioning to the man with her, "is *Duhubite Mumbichi,* Black Owl, my husband. We want you to know we have sought the *Boha,* our Great Spirit Father that He may give you strength in your vengeance battle."

Black Owl nodded and added, "If he takes your life, then I will seek vengeance for our child and her father and mother," nodding to his woman.

Ezra interjected, "If he defeats Spirit Bear, then I will fight. Walker killed my sister, the sister of my woman," nodding toward Dove.

"Whoa, hold on, both of you. You're acting like I'm already dead! That ain't gonna happen. Neither one of you will have to fight cuz that murderin' snake will be done with!" declared Gabe, shaking his head.

Ezra chuckled, "I know that!" as he turned to face the gathering crowd. He looked back at his friend as Gabe slipped the tomahawk and pistol from his belt and held them out for Ezra. The men walked side by side, Wolf beside Gabe, toward the circle to face the *aigwahni* or chief, Holder of Badgers. Beside him stood the three elders. The chief stepped forward, motioned to Moon Walker to come forward and as the two combatants stood angled toward one another and the chief, Holder of Badgers spoke, "This is a fight of vengeance." He had lifted his voice for all to hear and continued, "It has been said that Moon Walker has killed four Shoshone, two women, one elder, and one young woman. This was not done in battle and was not done to defend himself. Spirit Bear, as the husband of the first woman killed, has demanded his right to vengeance. They will fight to the death!"

He looked at the two men before him. Moon Walker stood with a breech cloth and leggings, but no tunic or shirt. He was broad shouldered and well-muscled, his chest deep and his arms tensed. An engraved silver band marked the uppermost part of his left bicep, two feathers hung from a scalplock and dangled behind his head. His long black hair hung in two braids over his shoulders, tufts of orange dyed rabbit fur decorating the ends. A black smudge showed across his forehead, a mark made by the shaman as he chanted his prayer for purity. His arms were folded across his chest and he glared at Gabe, cocking one eyebrow up to show his disdain.

Gabe was about a half hand taller, his long dark blonde hair held behind his neck with a rawhide tie. He wore a full set of buckskins and moccasins, made and decorated with beads and dyed quills by Pale Otter, that fit his lean frame closely. Although the buckskin would give his opponent something to grab in a close match, they would also give a little protection.

"Show your knives!" demanded the chief, and each man displayed their chosen knife in their open palms. Gabe's was the precision crafted Flemish knife with the inlaid and carved handle, butt and guard. The blade was of Damascus steel as were the swords of the Crusades and held an exceptionally sharp edge. Moon Walker's knife was a typical handmade knife, but instead of a flint blade, his had a steel blade, probably garnered from a French trader. After visually examining the knives, the chief looked up at the men, then nodded and stepped back.

Moon Walker quickly stepped away and dropped into a fighter's crouch, holding his knife in his right hand, blade up. Gabe also stepped back but he stood in a casual stance, grinning at the moves of Walker. As the Indian side stepped, slowly working his way around the circle, staring at Gabe, he growled, "You have lied! I will kill you, take your scalp while you still breathe, and stuff it in your mouth so you will never lie again!"

Gabe countered his moves, but was showing a relaxed attitude, chuckling at the man who was trying to frighten him with his words and the sweeping motion of his knife hand. Suddenly Moon Walker lunged forward with a stabbing motion aimed at Gabe's side, but the long, lean blonde sucked in his gut and stepped back just enough and parried the move with a downward slice of his knife across his wrist that drew first blood. Moon Walker jumped back, swiping sideways as he moved, the tip of the blade catching a bit of fringe at the sleeve of Gabe's tunic. Gabe had dropped into a crouch and held his knife loosely in his right hand, blade up, as he watched the eyes of Walker. The men circled one another, Walker repeatedly moving his knife side to side, focusing on the movement of Gabe.

Walker screamed, and with one leg outstretched, he stomped at the dirt to try to deflect Gabe's attention, and lunged forward with his knife extended, but Gabe sidestepped and used his foot in a sweeping motion to jerk the leg from under Walker and drop him to his back. But he did not press his advantage and the agile Walker rolled away, and sprang to his feet, dirt covering his already sweating body. He unconsciously brushed at the dirt on his stomach and Gabe lunged, but pulled up his thrust and stepped aside as Walker parried the thrust and swept his knife up attempting to disembowel Gabe. But his thrust was short, and Gabe knocked the blade aside and again parried with a cutting blow to the man's upper arm. But the cut was not deep, although it did draw blood and did more to anger the man than injure him.

"White man! Fight me! You do nothing but dance! You are afraid!" snarled Moon Walker, sweeping his knife side to side. He then tossed it back and forth between hands, watching the eyes of his opponent.

Gabe grinned, chuckled, "Moon Walker, no man is afraid of a woman killer! You're not only a woman killer, you could not do it until her hands were tied and you had a tether on her, then you threw her to the bear so you could run away like a scared rabbit! No one is afraid of you!"

Walker lifted his knife above his shoulder as he charged toward Gabe, screaming as he moved. His left hand was stretched toward him, but Gabe was ready and at the last instant, stepped to his right and brought up his knee to strike Walker in his gut, bending him over, then Gabe brought his left elbow down on the man's back, breaking a rib with the blow. He could have easily brought his knife down into the man's back, but he stepped away and let him fall to the ground. Walker instantly came to his feet, knife still in his hand and he charged again. Gabe feinted to the right again but moved to his left and tossed his knife from his right hand to his left. He caught Walker's knife hand with his left, catching Walker's knife on the hilt of his own, then brought his right fist from the ground and buried it in the solar plexus of the Indian, knocking the wind out of him and making him step back, bent over.

Walker glared up at Gabe who stood casually to the side, watching. With a quick glance at his wounds, Walker saw the blood trickling from the upper arm, but was unconcerned. He stood, staring at Gabe, and then dropped into his crouch and started circling again. Gabe watched his knife hand and his eyes, anticipating his moves. Commonly, when someone throws a knife, he will hold it by the tip of the blade, but a full grip with the blade forward shows the intention of a stab or thrusting cut, with the grip showing the blade down, an overhead stab. Walker held the blade as if he was ready to thrust forward, or cut in a sideways move, but he surprised Gabe as he twisted his arm and raised the knife as he lunged and reached to grab Gabe's tunic.

Gabe reached high to grab Walker's wrist and stepped into the charge. He caught the man's wrist in an iron grip, thrust his right shoulder into his chest and using the momentum of his charge, bent him backwards over his hip and threw him to the ground. Gabe drove his knee into the Indian's side and felt another rib break under his weight. Walker grunted as Gabe twisted his arm back further, making him drop his knife to the ground. Gabe suddenly stood, kicked Walker's knife away, and upended his own knife, catching it by the blade, and threw it to stick in the sod at Ezra's feet.

Moon Walker stared with a furrowed brow that showed his confusion. Why would this man throw away his knife, no warrior would do that? His anger flared as he thought the man was mocking him, and he breathed deep, flexing his muscles as he shouted, "You fool! Now I will break you in two!" He dropped into his stance, circled a few steps, then charged directly at Gabe. As Gabe stepped back, his foot rolled on a stone and he lost his balance, falling backward just as Walker hit him in the chest with his shoulder and wrapped his arms around him, driving him to the ground.

The full weight of the man drilled into his chest, driving the air from his lungs, and Gabe struggled for a breath. Walker sat up, straddling Gabe's chest, and put both hands at his throat, pushing forward with all his strength. But Gabe's hips were free, and he brought his feet up, bucked with his hips as he slapped both open palms to the man's ears, and thrust up with his shoulders, knocking the Indian aside. Gabe quickly rolled away and jumped to his feet, still struggling for air, and glared at the war leader as he too stood.

Gabe moved a little slower, gasping for air, and Walker charged. Gabe had his head down slightly, faking his weakness, and bent a little at his waist, but as Walker charged with his arms outstretched,

Gabe knew his intention was to grasp him and bend him backwards, but Gabe stepped back with his right foot, catching the charge with his left hip, and ducked under Walker's arm as he rolled him over his hip and threw him face down in the dirt. Again, Gabe stepped back and allowed his opponent to rise to his feet. Gabe stood, arms at his side, flexing his fists, and grinning at Walker.

The Indian was incensed, knowing the white man was playing with him, and his anger drove him to charge again, screaming and shaking his head, arms outstretched to grasp him like an angry grizzly. But Gabe dropped into a one-legged crouch, spinning on one heel as the man charged, and with a roundhouse sweep with his free leg, swept the legs from under Walker, dropping him to his back, knocking his wind out.

Walker rolled to his stomach, came to hands and knees, and glared at Gabe. He looked around the circle, saw one of his men squatted at the edge, holding his knife before him. Walker looked, nodded, and the man tossed the knife. Walker swept it up and lunged to his feet. His eyes flared wide, and he charged at Gabe, his knife hand rising for an overhand stab. Gabe dropped into a slight crouch, arms outstretched, and as Walker came near, Gabe suddenly rose, spinning away from the charge, but catching the upraised arm in both hands, and with a quick drop, flipped Walker end over end to drop on his back in the dirt, his knife in Gabe's hand.

Gabe stepped back, hands on his knees as he sucked air, and watched Walker slowly come to his feet. Gabe threw Walker's knife to stick it in the ground next to his by Ezra's feet. It was then Gabe noticed Dove was struggling to hold Wolf back and Ezra was leaning on his war club. He frowned at the thought but turned back to his opponent. He looked at Walker, "Now, woman killer, murderer of old men and women, you will pay the price of your cowardice and treachery."

The enraged Walker, now somewhat more wary, began to circle again. He knew he was stronger than this white man, but the way he fought he could not understand. But he knew he had to kill him, somehow, or he would be killed. But no man could kill him. He was Moon Walker, war leader of the Bannock! No one had ever lasted in a battle with him. Now, he would get rid of this white man! He feinted a charge, but the white man did nothing but grin. He had to get him in his arms, then he could crush the life out of him! He feinted with another lunge, then stepped to the side and charged.

When he came, his hands were low, hip high, and he was in a low crouch, but he charged with force. Gabe recognized the move, grinned, because this is what he was waiting for and expected. He too dropped, and as the Indian rushed toward him, he knew Walker expected him to try to move to one side or the other, but Gabe held his ground. At the last instant, Gabe grabbed Walker's right wrist, first with one hand then the other, and twisted to the side, letting his momentum carry him past, but Gabe held the wrist, brought it down then up behind Walker's back, and drove his arm up toward his neck. The sudden shove drove Walker forward, but he stumbled and caught his footing, yet Gabe thrust up on the arm and twisted it from the socket at his shoulder, sending stabbing pain up the man's shoulder and to his neck. Gabe held his grip, and as Walker struggled to keep his feet, Gabe pushed again, and the cracking sound of breaking bone caused the bystanders to gasp as Walker screamed in pain.

But Gabe did not release him, "Tell everyone you killed my woman!"

Walker groaned, trying to breathe, gritting his teeth and snarling, but he refused to talk. Gabe shoved and drove him into the dirt. Walker's arm was unusable, and Gabe thrust his knee into the man's back, grabbed his scalplock and jerked his head back. He nodded to Ezra and caught the thrown knife as it tumbled through the air. He cut the man's scalplock off, tossing it aside. He grabbed one of the braids, jerking the Indian's head back and put the knife at his throat. "I could cut your throat now like you did to my woman! Tell the people you are a coward and you killed my woman!"

But Walker would not speak, he tried to move

beneath Gabe, but was kept face down in the dirt by the knee in his back and the knife beside his face. Gabe cut the braid off, tossed it aside and grabbed the other, again jerking the man's head back. He cut off the second braid and tossed it away. He knew the man's shorn hair would mark him for all people to see he had been bested, but that was not enough. He still wanted vengeance.

Suddenly a scream came from the circle and the warrior that had thrown the knife to Walker, was charging with a raised tomahawk. But Gabe heard the voice of Ezra shout, "Duck!" and Gabe dropped his head as the war club swished over his head and back. A gasp came from the crowd as the massive war club, halberd blade forward, connected with the charging warrior. The blade took him in the throat and the momentum of his charge, and the swing of the war club decapitated the man and his body fell behind Gabe's feet, legs flopping, as the head tumbled to roll to the feet of the shaman.

Ezra stepped back and Gabe stood astraddle of Walker. Gabe looked down at the defeated Walker, wanting to slit his throat with the knife he held at his side, but the words, *"Vengeance is mine, I will repay,"* haunted his consciousness and he knew he could not do it, he had defeated and shamed the man and he would stop at that. He stepped away, and with a glance back, saw Walker struggling to his feet. Walker stood, looking down at the body of his warrior friend, a confused and angry expression on his face. He turned and glowered at Gabe's back, then stepped to the side of a warrior and snatched the tomahawk from his belt. He turned, one arm dangling at his side, then charged toward Gabe with hawk raised overhead. Dove shouted, "Behind you!" Gabe spun on his heel to see the man charging, he flipped his knife to catch it by the blade, but before he could throw it, a tomahawk whistled past and the blade was buried in the forehead of Walker, dropping him in death to the ground. Gabe looked around, saw Black Owl standing, spread legged, glaring at the dead body of Walker, and knew *he* had thrown the hawk.

27 / Resolution

Dove and Yellow Bird had taken the horses to Bird's lodge and tethered them nearby. When the group returned, Bird asked, "I have prepared a meal for all. You must eat." Gabe was weary, but hungry and a quick glance to Ezra showed his usual smile whenever food was mentioned. As the men were seated on blankets near the cookfire, two boys sat nearby, looking at the visitors. Black Owl pointed to the boys with his chin, "Our sons, Badger and Turtle." The older boy, Badger, appeared to be about ten or eleven summers, and the younger, Turtle, about eight. They wore breechcloths and moccasins, hair hanging in loose braids, and both had spirited eyes and their expressions showed curiosity.

Turtle leaned toward Ezra, "Why are you like the buffalo?"

Ezra chuckled, "Why are you like the turtle?" grinning at the boy.

The boy leaned back, surprised, and answered, "Because I move slow, but careful. I have a hard shell," he beat on his chest, "and I like the water!"

"But the turtle can put his head in his shell, can you?"

The boy frowned, thinking, tucked his chin to his chest and answered, "No! No man can do that!"

"So, in some ways you are like the turtle, and other ways you are not?"

The boy thought for a moment, then with a slow nod, he answered a little quieter, "Yes."

Ezra nodded, "My name is Black Buffalo. I was named for the buffalo because my hair," he put his hand to his head and his chin whiskers, "is like the buffalo. And I have big muscles," he flexed his arms and pushed out his chest, scowling, "like the big bull buffalo. But also, because my skin," he held his arm out to the boy and pinched a bit of skin, "is the same color as the buffalo." He paused, then nodded to the boy, "Your skin is like your father's, and mine is like my father's. Where we," nodding to Gabe, "come from, there are many people like me, and there are some that are different than both of us."

"Oh," replied Turtle, sitting back.

Black Owl chuckled, "Just like there are differences between our people and many other people of the plains, like the Blackfoot, the Crow, the Nez Perce, and others, there are differences between the people in other places too."

Ezra nodded to Gabe, "He is called Spirit Bear because in the mountains far to the north, there are bear
that have the same color of hair as his, and sometimes
he is called Claw of the Spirit Bear, because he uses a
bow and arrow and can shoot his arrows farther than
any warrior you know. I have seen him use his arrows to
kill Blackfoot as far away as," he paused to look around,
"the other side of the river, there," he nodded toward the
trees at the river that were about a hundred yards away,
and across the river would be much further.

The boys looked, as did their father, then looked back
at Ezra and Gabe, doubt showing on their faces. Ezra
continued, "And he has arrows that scream like an eagle!"

Their eyes flared and again they looked from Ezra
to Gabe. Coyote said, "No man can shoot an arrow
that far, can they Father?"

Black Owl paused, looking at his boys, and slowly
answered, "You are right to question what you do not
know, and you were right to ask me that question. If
you had said that to Black Buffalo, it would be an insult
to suggest he was lying. Now, I have never seen anyone
send an arrow that far and hit anything or kill anything,
but, there are many things that I have not seen. If you
think that something is not true because you have not
seen it, is a mistake. But to question is to learn."

Turtle looked to Gabe as he asked, "Would you
show us how you can send an arrow that far?" he

paused only an instant before he added, "And the arrow that screams like an eagle?"

Gabe chuckled, looked at the women and saw Dove smiling at the men and their talk, then he looked at the boys, "Yes, but first, we must eat. Your mother has worked hard to prepare that food. Aren't you hungry?"

Coyote looked from the men to the food, then to his brother, and said, "No, we are not hungry." He jumped up, motioned to his brother, and the boys took off running into the village, probably to see their friends. But Gabe guessed it was to tell the tales of what they learned about these strange men that are visiting with his family, and about what they would soon see at the hand of the white man.

Gabe and Ezra watched the boys run away, then Gabe turned to Black Owl, "You have some fine boys, there."

Black Owl nodded, chuckled, "Turtle is as his name, but he thinks about things and that is good. Coyote will be a strong warrior, but he is too quick to act sometimes. He will need to learn to be patient."

"But they are boys to be proud of, and I'm sure you and Bird will do a fine job with them." He looked a little wistfully in the direction the boys had gone, remembering the times he and Otter had talked about having children. He dropped his head and stared at the rocks at his feet until Dove brought carved platters of food to him and Ezra.

He looked down at the platter to see a sizeable

trout that covered the top of the platter. As he looked around, he saw the same on each platter. He knew there were some tribes that refused to eat fish, but he had always enjoyed them, especially the trout found in the mountain streams. Although unfamiliar with the different strains of the trout, the one before him was a golden trout, only found in the streams in the higher elevations. He carefully peeled the skin back to reveal the pale flaky meat and picked at it, taking each tender morsel and enjoying the flavor. The meat readily came from the thin bones and soon all that was left was the hair thin bones and the skin, which Gabe tossed to the waiting Wolf, who made it disappear without so much as a chew. It was a tasty treat and he soon finished his plate, handing it back to a smiling Dove. "Thank you! That was delicious!" commented Gabe, looking at both Bird and Dove. The women smiled, nodded, and tended to the work of cleaning up after the men.

Gabe leaned back, content with his full belly, and looked around. He was missing his coffee but knew that was a drink that was foreign to the people, and he smiled at the memory of Otter always ensuring he had his coffee. Ezra interrupted his reverie, "Didn't you promise the boys somethin'?"

Gabe looked at him, grinned, "Yeah, guess I did."

"Well, here they come, and they ain't alone!"

Gabe looked where Ezra pointed to see the two

youngsters, followed by a group of at least a dozen more, as well as a handful of warriors. But the surprising one was Holder of Badgers, the chief, and the shaman, Two Moons.

"Ohoh, are we in trouble?" asked Gabe, glancing to Black Owl.

"No, but with the stories those boys told . . ." he answered, rising from his seat to greet the chief and shaman. Gabe and Ezra also stood, but Gabe turned to go to his gear and retrieve his Mongol Bow and the quiver of arrows. When he returned, the others were talking and the chief was asking questions about the tale of the boys, "We have not known your boys to be less than truthful, but when we heard what they were saying, we had to come see," explained the chief.

Black Owl turned back to look at Gabe, then spoke to the chief, "Black Buffalo did say that Claw of the Spirit Bear could shoot an arrow across the river. He also said Spirit Bear could shoot an arrow that screams like an eagle."

The chief and the others nearby frowned, looked past Black Owl at Gabe. The chief grunted and nodded, then stepped closer to where Gabe was standing, ready to string the bow. Gabe but the tip of the bottom limb on the ground, stepped over it, hooked his right foot behind the nock that held the string, then using the strength of his entire body, he bent the bow back to slip the string into the top nock. He brought his left leg back and lifted the bow to show it to the chief.

As Gabe held the bow flat on his extended arms, the chief looked closely. It was unlike any bow he had ever seen. He carefully and gently touched the thin birch bark covering, and Gabe pointed out, "That layer is ram's horn, the next layer is a very strong wood, called bamboo, and the next is sinew. The layers are laminated and glued together with a glue made from fish." He pointed to the curves of the limbs, "This is what is called a 'recurve'," and ran his finger along the lines of the bow.

The chief looked up at Gabe, "What is it called?"

"This is a Mongol Bow. It is used by a tribe of people a long way from here. To get to their land, you would have to travel for a year and use a big boat on part of the journey."

"Did these Mongol people make this bow?"

"Yes. My father got it when we went on the long journey several years ago. I have used it since that time."

The chief lifted his head and looked at Gabe with a piercing gaze, and Gabe knew he was being judged by the man as to the truth of his words. Gabe nodded, "Let me show you."

He looked to Black Owl, "Does Coyote have a horse to cross the river and retrieve my arrows?" Before Owl could answer, the boy shouted, "I will get my horse!" and took off at a run.

Within moments, Coyote returned, and Gabe said,

"Go down there, stay on this side, but watch as the arrow goes over head and see where it falls. But don't go until after I shoot the second arrow."

Coyote looked from Gabe to his father, and with his father's nod, the boy gigged his mount into a run toward the river. As the boy rode, Gabe put the jade ring on his thumb, and nocked an arrow. When he stopped and turned back to wave, Gabe drew the bow to full draw, lifted it a bit, then let the arrow fly. It was an almost flat trajectory, which he did intentionally, to show the strength of the bow, and the long black arrow flew swiftly, crossed the river, and fell into the grass about forty or fifty yards beyond the river.

The youngsters and warriors all chattered and exclaimed about what they had witnessed, many saying they would not have believed if someone told them about an arrow going that far. Gabe slipped a whistler arrow from the quiver, nocked it and lifted the bow at a higher angle, drew it back and sent the arrow on its way. It immediately sounded its screaming whistle, and everyone gasped, eyes flaring, and as the whistle faded when the arrow completed its arch, the chatter was overwhelming as each one exclaimed to the other about what they heard.

The chief stepped closer and looked at the bow, then asked, "What makes the arrow sing?"

Gabe slipped another whistler from the quiver, held it before the chief, "It is nothing but a hollowed-out

bone, held to the shaft with glue and thin rawhide."
He lifted the arrow to his lips and blew through the
bone, making a faint sound to prove his point.

The chief grinned, looked at the bow and Gabe,
then asked, "I saw you hold the arrow with your
thumb, why?" He spoke of the unusual way Gabe
drew the string, using his thumb, with his two fingers
overlapping that provided a greater grip on the string.
Usually, an archer would use just his fingers, keeping
the nock of the arrow between the first and second
digit, giving a straighter release. But the greater draw
weight of the Mongol bow made that difficult.

"The strength of this bow requires more," explained Gabe, simply.

"Can I shoot this bow?" asked Holder of Badgers.

"If you want, but it is difficult. I can only do it because I have had it many years," explained Gabe as he
handed the bow to the chief. He slipped an arrow from
the quiver and handed it to the chief. Holder of Badgers
looked at the arrow, noted its length, then nocked it as
he lifted the bow. With the usual grip of three fingers,
he started to draw the bow, but was instantly surprised
as he struggled to draw it more that the breadth of a
hand. He released the tension, then looked at Gabe,
"I see. It is strong." He removed the arrow, handed
the bow back to Gabe and spoke softly, head slightly
ducked, "It is best I do not shame myself."

Gabe responded, "To master this bow takes years

for any man."

As the chief turned away, Coyote rode up and slipped down, triumphantly holding both arrows out to Gabe. He looked at the crowd as they turned back to the village, leaving in groups, all talking about what they had seen this strange white man do with his bow. Coyote looked at Gabe and asked, "Can I shoot your bow?"

Black Owl interjected, "No, you may not. Even Holder of Badgers could not shoot this bow. Spirit Bear said it takes many summers for anyone to learn to shoot this bow."

Gabe said, "Let's let him try, that way he'll understand." He looked at Coyote, said, "Stand here," he pointed to a spot close by, and when Coyote was in place. Gabe handed him the bow and said, "Now, grip it tightly here," pointing at the grip and his small fingers that wrapped around the large grip, "Now lift it, and with your three fingers, draw back the string."

"But there's no arrow," he pleaded.

Gabe chuckled, "If you can draw the string back to your ear, I'll give you an arrow to shoot"

Coyote grinned, extended his arm with the bow, and with all four fingers, tugged on the string. When it didn't move, he frowned, looked from Gabe to his father, both of whom were grinning, then tried again with so much force his face turned dark and the muscles in his neck stood out, but he could not draw the string an inch. He let out his breath, lowered the bow, looked at his father and said, "Can you draw it?"

"I'm not even going to try!" replied a chuckling Black Owl.

Gabe took the bow and went through his contortions to unstring the weapon, replaced it in the oiled case, and took it to his gear. When he returned, Ezra spoke, "I told Black Owl we have the lodge that belongs to Bird's mother and offered to bring it here, but he said that had already been settled with the women. So, I guess, like most native peoples, that lodge now belongs to Dove."

Gabe grinned, chuckled, "Good. At least she knows how to put one up, which is more'n what we could do."

"And, Owl and his family will be at the lodge tomorrow for some fresh venison steaks. So, I reckon we better go find some!"

Black Owl interjected, "Or, we might find some *bozheena*, or buffalo, if we go south early in the morning."

Both Gabe and Ezra grinned, looked at one another, then back to Owl, "We'll do it!" declared Ezra.

28 / Bozheena

The fog lay heavy in the valley like a downy blanket that muted all sounds and even slowed time. Gabe and Ezra's usual jaunt to a high place to spend the first moments of the day with their Maker, was stayed and they huddled around the fire in the midst of the tipi. The glow and warmth from the flames brought an unmistakable comfort and felt as though it sought to push back the mask of fog. Dove had a pot of coffee dancing at the edge of the coals, a pan with smoked meat, turnips, and cat-tail shoots simmering at the edge. A dutch oven sat covered hiding the promise of fresh cornbread. The men sat pensive, each immersed in his own thoughts, silently voicing their prayers and pondering the memories.

Gabe's quiet moments were filled with thoughts of Pale Otter, memories made and dreams unfulfilled. He sighed heavily as the weight of the past pressed hard upon him. He dropped his gaze to the fire, arched his back and stretched, then stood and went to the entry. He lifted the blanket flap, peering outside, and the downy fog moved slowly into the valley beyond. He heard a hail and stepped out to see the mounted Black Owl part the fog as if coming from a nether land. He reined up and leaned forward to greet Gabe. "I see you are waiting. But you are not ready." He grinned as he slipped to the ground.

Gabe chuckled, "This fog has us movin' a little slow this mornin', but Dove's got some vittles on the fire. Tether your horse and come inside, I think we could use a good meal 'fore we try to take a buffalo." He started to turn back to the lodge, but the fog stirred again, and Yellow Bird and the two boys rode up behind Black Owl and stopped. Gabe smiled, motioned them to come inside and flipped the blanket aside and ducked into the warm interior.

"We've got comp'ny," he announced as he stepped into the glow of the fire.

Dove was quick to answer, "Of course we do. You don't think I fixed all this just for you two, do you?"

***

The anxious hunters made short work of the meal and it was decided the women would stay in camp, but if they were needed with a travois or to help with the butchering, one of the boys would return for them. The boys were happy to be joining the men on the hunt, as the usual hunting parties of the men of the village seldom included young men, and then only those that were nearing manhood. Coyote was the oldest and he still had a couple summers to go before he would be accepted as part of a hunting party.

The usual grey of early morning was muted with the heavy fog, but all around them the wispy cloud was slowly turning a light grey, as the hunters left the camp behind. Black Owl, with Coyote and Turtle alongside, led the way. Gabe and Ezra trailed behind, with Gabe leading the blue roan for a packhorse. They pointed due south, following the middle fork river into the flat grassy plain. Shadows stood beside them, changing shapes as they moved and as the sun slowly rose to burn off the fog.

Black Owl led them on a twisting trail, which Gabe would later discover was due to the many bogs in the flats that held nothing but cattails, thin willows, and black mud overgrown with thin grasses, and if they were to try to step on the grassy mounds, it would disappear into the depths of the dark slimy mud. Gabe let Ebony have his head and the big wolf padded his way behind the others. The damp thick fog and the quiet morning let Gabe slip into his tranquil state of reflection and consideration. With the youngsters around, his thoughts were on family, the family he would never have with Pale Otter, and he remembered his younger sister, Gwyneth, and the times they had together. He wondered how she and her new husband, Hamilton Claiborne, were doing in the new seat of government, Washington. They had great dreams and plans, perhaps they had a family now and he was an uncle. He grinned at the thought and wondered if the one letter he sent by way of the passing trappers ever made it to her.

His thoughts turned to the fortune left him by his father and wondered if the other letter had reached the attorney that was to handle those affairs. He had asked that the funds be transferred to the bank in St. Louis, but then what? And what about Gwyneth? Shouldn't she share in the inheritance, although his father had chosen to leave it all to Gabriel? He shook his head, feeling the warmth of the rising sun on his cheek and he looked to see the fog breaking up and the sun barely pushing through the grey to make silhouettes of the eastern mountains.

A few moments more and Black Owl had brought them to a stop as he twisted around to watch the others draw close. The sun flared bright off their left shoulders but had risen enough to give detail to the plateau and its ridges. Black Owl pointed to a high rim rock edged mesa, "That is a buffalo jump my people have used many times before."

Gabe and Ezra looked to see a high wide flat-top

with a line of dun colored rimrock that marked the edge. Falling away from the rim were several piles of rock, but mostly a steep slope that eased as it fell to a narrow ravine at the bottom. The top of the flat was about three hundred feet above the bottom of the slope. Gabe looked at Owl, "Just what is a buffalo jump?"

Owl grinned, stepped down from his mount and stretched, prompting the others to follow suit, and he began to explain. "When the buffalo come in the late time of greening, there are big herds. And in the time of my youth, our people did not have horses, or very many horses. And to take a buffalo was hard. The hunters would cover themselves with the hides of coyotes or buffalo calves, and crawl close to get a shot with a bow or to run and throw or thrust a lance. But the herd would run away and very few were taken." He paused, walked to a boulder to take a seat, then continued, "We learned to drive the herd, although sometimes one of our fast runners would act as a buffalo calf and try to get them to follow, but we would drive the herd by waving blankets and shouting. We would stack rocks along the way to hide behind, then jump up and wave the blankets or hides and shout to keep them going where we wanted. Then, up there," he pointed to the flat plateau above the rimrock, "we would drive them down that narrow slope, and out to the end of the rocks. They would be running all out and only those in the lead could see, there was so much dust, and the others would keep pushing, until many and sometimes all, of the buffalo would run off the cliff and fall to their deaths." He paused as he pictured it in his memory, then dropped his eyes, and looked back at the others.

"Down below, the waiting warriors and the women would cut the throats of those that were not dead, and when all was quiet, then they would start the butchering. Other bands would help us in the drive and there would be meat for everyone. It would be followed by a great feast and everybody would be happy that we would have meat for the winter."

He looked at his boys, then to Gabe and Ezra, "There are still many bones there, but we haven't done that for some seasons. Now, we hunt from horseback and take them, and do not take as many, leaving the rest to return the next summer. That is why our bands break up into smaller villages."

"Have your people already had your summer hunt?" asked Ezra.

"Yes. Most are still busy smoking the meat, curing the hides, and more. We have had a good hunt, but there are plenty buffalo for you."

***

When they started out again, they held close to the river on the west edge of the valley that spanned about

a mile or more wide, showing wide meadows with
deep grasses that slowly waved in the morning breeze.
What had been a boggy bottom, now was expansive
grassland and a patchwork of grassy meadows and
dryer buffalo grass and bunch grass interspersed with
cacti and sage that rested in the lowlands between the
round top buttes on the west and the flat plateaus and
mesas on the east. The end of the long valley seemed
to rise up to meet the distant mountains that still held
patches of white showing the glaciers that would keep
their place throughout the summer months and be
added to with the following winter's snows. Timber
covered hills stood between the rolling lands and the
mountain peaks, standing like guards over the riches
of the high country.

Yet it was from the high country that vast herds
of wapiti would migrate to the warm meadows of
the lower climes, often grazing shoulder to shoulder
with moose, deer and pronghorns. While their usual
summer companions, big horn sheep and mountain
goats, stayed in the high country. The river they
followed pointed a crooked finger to the cleft in the
mountains to tell of the home of its headwaters. It was
a beautiful and fertile country, abounding in game
and the hidden riches buried by the Creator.

Owl had them near a patch of scraggly cottonwood
that hung on the bank of the river when he held up
a hand to stop them. He slipped down, motioned for

them to come alongside, and as they neared, he pointed to the wide meadow before them. They dropped to their knees as they looked past the low branches of the nearest ponderosa, standing alone among the cottonwoods, to see a sizable herd of elk. The sun had burned off the fog, except a few whiffs near the river, but the meadow was clear. The men collectively frowned as each one discovered what they were seeing. This was a band of bulls. Some young enough to be sprouting their first single prong of a velvet covered antler, and others already showing a massive but still growing rack as was evidenced by the velvet that covered the crowning antlers. The big ones were already strutting around, lifting their heads, flexing their neck muscles, rocking the tines back and forth. One big bull stretched out his neck and with mouth wide to show his teeth, squealed and coughed, sides heaving with the effort. It wasn't the usual bugle done in the fall when the bulls challenge one another, it was simply a bull making himself known.

With the velvet on, antlers still growing, none of the bulls were sparring, which would come later in the summer, due to the racks still being tender and thick with blood flowing as they grew. This just appeared to be a gathering of bulls, while the cows were off by themselves and tending their young. They lazily grazed through the grass, some working their way to the water, but most busy with filling their stomachs.

Owl stepped back into the trees, looked at the others, "Do you want to take one of these?"

"I like elk meat!" declared Ezra, grinning.

"With this herd here, I think they might have crowded out the buffalo. But the buffalo could be back in the hills, there," pointing to the southwest.

Gabe looked at Ezra, back to Owl, "Elk meat suits me." He glanced at the boys and asked, "Have either of you ever killed an elk?"

Coyote looked excited as he answered, "No, but I want to!"

Turtle shook his head, but his eyes were wide, and a smile painted his face.

Gabe looked at Owl, "Have either of them ever shot a rifle? Or have you?"

Owl's eyebrows lifted, "No, I have not shot a rifle and the boys have never seen one."

Gabe grinned, "Would it be alright if they had a go at it?"

Owl grinned and nodded, and the boys excitedly hopped and started to clap, but a stern look from their father stilled them instantly. They stood together, watching every move made by Gabe and Ezra as the men went to their mounts and slipped the rifles from the scabbards. Ezra motioned for Turtle to come close and Gabe stepped before Coyote and his father. Gabe began by explaining, "This is called a Ferguson Rifle because of, well, because of how it works. That one," nodding to the rifle in Ezra's hands, "is called a Lancaster Rifle. Now, let me show you how this works and we'll see if you can take an elk with it." Coyote's eyes grew large and he looked from Gabe to Owl and back again. He grinned widely and Turtle was the same with Ezra. Both men showed how the rifle was loaded, but focused more on how to hold it, aim it, and when to squeeze the trigger.

"Now, we'll work our way close, pick out the one we want, and wait till the other one signals he is ready before we shoot," instructed Gabe. He loosely cradled the rifle in his hand at his side, and with a nod to Ezra, the men started in opposite directions. Ezra and Turtle were to work through the brush at river's edge to get further upstream and closer to a small group of young bulls. Gabe, Owl, and Coyote would move behind a line of brush that extended out into the meadow to find a position and a target.

Owl led the way to a slight depression with some sage brush at the edge to provide cover. They were near the north east edge of the band of bulls and Gabe pointed out a good-sized young bull with a single stub of antlers that stood about a foot high. He was grazing, and seldom lifted his head to look around at the others. Gabe whispered, "Now, like I said, pull it into your shoulder and line up the sights. That single blade in the front between the buckhorns at the back. When you're ready, bring the hammer all the way back, and lay your finger alongside the front trigger." He watched as the boy did as directed, breathing excitedly. "Now, wait till I signal and hear the signal back from Black Buffalo." He lifted his head and pursed his lips to give the high pitched whee-ah whistle of the whiskey jack. Instantly came the response from across the flat near the river's edge. And within moments, both rifles sounded, one almost an echo of the other. Gabe watched as the big rifle bucked in the hands of the boy, spitting smoke out to the side and from the barrel. The boy had been on one knee, the other used as a rest for his elbow, and he was rocked back, almost falling to the ground before Gabe put the flat of his hand at his back to hold him. He was so startled he looked at the rifle, then to Gabe and his father, before remembering he had shot at an elk. He struggled to get his balance, and looked in the direction of the elk, to see the animal on its side, legs kicking for an instant, then stilled.

The rest of the herd sprung like they were connected with a long tether, every animal jerking to the side and bounding away toward the narrow mouth of the canyon that birthed the river. Within moments, the meadow was empty, and Gabe stood, looking in the direction of Ezra and saw him standing and waving with the younger boy at his side.

Coyote stood, holding the rifle out to Gabe, then put his left hand to his right shoulder and frowned,

"I did not think it would hit me!" he declared. Gabe and Owl chuckled at the boy, his father rubbing the boy's head, and Gabe said, "But look how hard it hit the elk!" and pointed to the downed bull. While Owl and Coyote started field dressing the bull, Gabe reloaded and looked up to see Ezra and Turtle leading the horses toward them. Gabe stood and waited for them to come near as Ezra said, "Came close, but not close enough!" He grinned at the boy, "But he gave it a good try!"

Turtle grinned and handed the reins to Ezra as he ran forward to join his father and brother at the carcass of the downed elk. With everyone helping, the butchering was quickly done, and the meat wrapped in the hide and most packed aboard the blue roan. But it was more than one horse could handle and a smaller bundle was strapped on behind the successful hunter, Coyote. The boys rode together, chattering all the way about their great experience, one that most of the other youngsters would never have or if they did it would be many years in the future.

They were headed back to the camp, the sun now high overhead, Owl and Ezra riding side by side in the lead, followed close behind by the boys, and Gabe, Wolf, and the packhorse trailing the group. Suddenly, Ezra stopped, motioned to Owl, and the men slipped from their horses with nothing more than a motion to the boys and Gabe. The boys waited as Gabe drew closer, then he motioned for them to dismount as did he, holding tight to the reins of their horses, craning around to see what had piqued the interest of Owl and Ezra.

Suddenly a rifle barked and bucked, a puff of smoke showed above the brush, and Gabe snatched his rifle from the scabbard to stand ready. But the call from Ezra, "Come ahead on!" prompted them to round the point of bushes and find Owl standing triumphantly over the carcass of a nice doe mule deer. He held Ezra's rifle, and was grinning broadly, relieved to not be outdone by his boys.

29 / Traders

"Do you know these traders?" asked Black Owl, sitting beside his woman near the fire. The afternoon had been spent working on the meat and hides from the elk and deer, with most going to Owl and Bird, but a good-sized bundle would be for Gabe and company. After the evening meal, the group was talking and learning more about one another and their people.

"We met them, talked for a little, but haven't traded with 'em yet, have you?" asked Gabe.

"We traded a few pelts to them for some beads and things. Bird likes the metal needles for beading and making our things," he reached at his waist and brought out a knife, "and I traded for a new knife with the metal blade." He held it out for Gabe and Ezra to see, obviously proud of his trade. Any item of metal was a rarity in the mountains where white men were seldom found, and traders were scarce. The natives usually crafted their weapons from materials at hand, flint the most common material for knives, each hand crafted by a village flint knapper to a fine edge. But flint, in large pieces, was easily broken, and the discovery of the metal bladed knives of the traders and trappers made them greatly sought after by the natives.

Gabe handed his knife to Owl to examine and his eyes grew wide and a smiled crossed his face as he handled the beautifully crafted Flemish weapon. Gabe explained, "That knife was made by a craftsman many years ago, and the steel in the blade was also used to make the swords of warriors that fought in the land far from here."

"What is a 'sword'?" asked Coyote, looking at the knife in his father's hands.

Gabe lifted his eyebrows as he realized even the word was foreign to the native people and to describe it would be difficult, but he began, "It's like a very long knife," he held his hands apart, "with a blade this long!" He saw the expression on both Owl's face and that of his son. He stood, and taking the knife back from Owl, he tried to demonstrate, "It has a handle like this, but the blade is used, well, like a spear. The warrior drives it into his enemy with a thrust like this," he made a quick step forward, extending his knife hand straight forward, "and with the long blade, he can strike the enemy down. But if he misses, with the long blade, he can slash back like this," and made a move as if he held a blade, "and cut him very badly, maybe even cut his arm so deep, he won't be able to fight." He sat back down, "But it's just like another weapon, and is only as effective as the man using it."

Coyote looked at his father, "His people," nodding to Gabe, "are very strange, but they have so many weapons! Have you known others that have weapons like Spirit Bear and Black Buffalo?"

Owl nodded, "I have seen others with weapons like Bear and Buffalo, but none were as good as what they have," he nodded toward Gabe and Ezra, "but it's not the weapon, its who has it and how they use it."

Coyote looked at his father with a slight frown, then nodded his head and looked back at Gabe. "It is good that you are a friend to our people. It is too bad that Moon Walker did what he did."

Gabe dropped his eyes for a moment, then looked back to Coyote and to Turtle, "Like your father said, it is not the weapon, but the man. You have shown yourself to be a good young man, and with your father to guide you, I am sure you too will be a good man."

Coyote and Turtle, smiled, looking around at the others and especially their mother to see if she heard what this great warrior had said about her sons. Bird was watching and when her sons looked to her, she smiled and nodded slightly, her pride in her boys evident.

"We're gonna be talkin' to the traders tomorrow, is there anything you would like to get?" asked Ezra, looking from Owl to Bird. He noticed Bird's eyes quickly go to the Dutch Oven that Dove had used, but she dropped her eyes without looking at Ezra. He remembered when she had prepared the meal for them the day before, he saw no pot or pan of metal, which was common among the native people that had not been visited by a trader with such items.

"I have a few more pelts to trade. Perhaps I will go with you," replied Black Owl.

Dove looked at Yellow Bird, reached out to touch her arm, "We will go also," and smiled, prompting a smile from Bird.

"Can we go too, father?" asked Turtle, beating Coyote to the asking, but garnering a nodding grin from his brother.

"Do you have anything to trade?" asked Owl.

The boys looked to one another, then to their father, long faces showing, and shook their heads.

"It will be good for you to learn about traders and what they do. You will come," spoke Owl with a very stoic expression, showing himself as a stern father and teacher. But the others knew he was not what he portrayed, and often doted on the boys unnecessarily.

***

Black Owl and his family returned to the lodge of Grey Dove and the men shortly after first light. Gabe was walking down the slope that rose behind their camp and held the point of rocks that Gabe had chosen for his morning time with the Lord. Ezra had selected another knob of the hill and had already returned to camp. Gabe waved at the family as Ezra greeted the four, "Welcome, welcome." He looked at the boys, "Ready for a big day of dickerin' with the traders?"

The boys frowned, looked at their father and back to Black Buffalo, "What is 'dickerin'?" asked Coyote, slipping from his mount and sliding to the ground. He turned to Ezra as he stood, waiting for an explanation.

"Uh, well, that's when you talk to the trader about whatever it is you want to trade for, and after you talk about it, you and the trader finally agree on what you will trade and what he will give you in trade."

Coyote lifted his head slowly, considering what the man said, and understanding, smiled and answered, "I see."

Ezra looked to Bird, motioned toward the tipi to indicate Dove was inside, then turned to Owl, just as Gabe came into camp. Ezra looked at Gabe, "So, just what are we gonna be tradin' for?"

"Oh, I dunno. He said they might have some coffee to spare, how 'bout that for starters?" asked Gabe.

Ezra grinned, "Can always use coffee, that's for certain."

"Mainly, I just want to get the news of what's been goin' on since we left Philadelphia. It's been a few years and I think we'd do well to catch up on things, don't you?" asked Gabe.

Ezra pursed his lips, raised his eyebrows and nodded, agreeing.

Alexander Henry, David Thompson and two other men were seated near a fire away from the wall tents and looked up when Gabe and company drew near. Henry stood, smiled, and extended his hand, "Well, I wondered when you'd stop back by and get that coffee you were so anxious about!" He stepped forward and shook hands with Gabe, Ezra, and Black Owl. He looked at Owl, "We've done a little trading before, haven't we?"

"Yes, I brought my boys and my woman to see what you have," replied Owl.

"Good, good. Well, let's go to the tent and tables, see if there's something you need." Henry glanced at Owl who had a bundle hanging at his back. "Got some more pelts?"

"Yes."

Henry looked to Gabe and Ezra, "You look like you want more'n coffee, what can I do for you?"

Gabe grinned, "Oh, we need the coffee, but I'd like to chat a spell, catch up on the happenings in the world, if you don't mind. It's been a few years since we've had any news and don't know much about how the rest of the world is getting by without us!"

Henry looked to his partner, Thompson, and motioned him to tend to the others and then motioned for Gabe to have a seat on a chest outside the wall tent. The men sat opposite one another and Henry asked, "Well, what can I tell you?"

Gabe chuckled, "We left Philadelphia in '95, and anything of importance after that, I'm all ears."

"Hmmm, well, let me think. Let's see, uh, did you know about the Treaty of Madrid?"

"No."

"It was between U.S. and Spain, set up the boundaries of the Spanish colonies, territories, and the States. Then, oh yeah, another state came into the U.S., Tennessee became the sixteenth state!" he grinned at the thought, knowing it was no concern of his since he was a Canadian. But he continued, "Uh, part of the Jay Treaty gave the city of Detroit to the U.S. from Britain, then John Adams became president, and Thomas Jefferson is vice-president. Oh, and America and France have been at war, sort of, mainly on the seas. The French have been taking American ships, then America rose up against 'em and took eighty-four French ships, and that didn't sit too well with the French.

"Then a little popinjay name o' Napoleon, was made First Consul of France and he put a stop to the French raids." He paused, thinking about events that stood out in his memory, "George Washington died, just last year. Let's see, oh yeah, the congress of the

U.S. met for the first time in Washington, D.C. And Jefferson tried to get a law passed to outlaw slavery. It failed by one vote! But they did get it outlawed in the Northwest territory." He leaned forward, elbows on his knees, "Not much else, 'ceptin' things about the fur trade. Choteau in St. Louis is gettin' more involved, Hudson's Bay's still goin' strong, even though the fightin' between France and the U.S. is calmin' down. Northwest Company still doin' trades and such. Reckon the fur trade will get even busier in the comin' years."

"So, is St. Louis a busy town?" asked Gabe, trying to be casual with his question.

"Ain't been there, but from what folks are sayin', it's a growin' town, and becoming a hub for fur trading. Last I heard, there's more'n two thousand people there."

"That *is* growing. We met Choteau a couple years back when we were with the Osage and he was startin' his tradin' post on the Verdigris. So, he's got a thriving trade, does he?"

"He does that. You thinkin' about goin' to St. Louis?"

Gabe dropped his eyes, looked toward the tent where the others were busy, then back at Henry, "Maybe. Got some business to tend to and I want to find out about my family."

"If you do, I recommend you go by way of the river," he nodded toward the Missouri River that formed from the confluence of the three forks. "It'll take you all the way, easier than overland. And, if you do, I've got a fine canoe that would do the job."

Gabe frowned, looked at Henry, "A canoe? Never thought about the river. Guess it would be easier." He paused a bit, looked toward the tent again, then back to Henry. "Let me think about it."

"Don't take too long. We're pullin' out in a couple days. We're headed overland to the northwest. We met some Kootenai that said there's a river that would take us all the way to the Pacific, but, it's too far to carry a canoe."

Gabe grinned and stood, turned to join the others at the trading table. His mind busy with thoughts of family, travel, and more.

30 / Decision

Gabe sat back, grinning at the excitement of the family of Black Owl. They had reaped a bounty with the
trader, unknowing about Gabe's deal with Alexander
Henry that added to their take. Henry had expressed to
Gabe his ambition of going to the northwest and taking
the river told about by the Kootenai, and that he was
not wanting to take the extra baggage of pelts and furs,
but the trades were necessary to make overtures with
the natives, contacts that could one day benefit him and
his trading partners greatly. When Gabe suggested it
would be easier to pack a few gold coins than bales of
fur, Henry's countenance changed considerably.

Now as he watched Black Owl's family, Gabe was
reminded of family Christmases back in Philadelphia
when he and his sister joyfully opened gifts and shared
the excitement with the others. The boys of Black Owl
had each bargained for a knife, Bird got her Dutch oven,

and Gabe gifted Black Owl with Pale Otter's rifle and accouterments. Yet as he watched the family he was also reminded once again of the dreams he and Otter shared about having a family, and his thoughts also turned to his sister, Gwyneth, far away in Washington. He sighed heavily as he stood and stretched, looking at the distant mountains and the fertile green valley.

Should he go to St. Louis and tend to the family business matters? Maybe there would be a letter from Gwyneth waiting, and if not, he could get one off to her. He looked at Ezra, who sat with the boys, talking about sharpening knives, and wondered what he would think about making the trip back to the world of the white man. He paused in his thoughts as he considered the problem of slavery and the threat it would be to his friend. The Fugitive Slave Act of 1793 had made things more difficult for free blacks. Even though it was passed to aid slave owners in the re-capture of their property, slave catchers would often take free men, claiming they were escaped slaves and the man had no recourse, it was the word of a white slave catcher against the black.

They had been confronted with that before and escaped the consequences. And now in the Spanish Louisiana territory, the Spanish had outlawed the taking of Natives as slaves, but there was no enforce-ment and Gabe and Ezra had seen the hazards of that as well. Even when they spent time with the Maroons, they saw the constant danger experienced by a person of color. Perhaps it would not be good for Ezra to go with him to St. Louis, and he caught himself as he realized his decision had already been made, he was going to St. Louis, even if he was to go by himself.

He had walked away from the others as he chased those thoughts in his mind, occasionally kicking at a stone to send it skipping into the water, picking up a random stick to toss it into the grass. All the while with Wolf walking at his side, patiently watching the man and detecting his pensive mood, but the big wolf stayed at his side. But how would he go? Should he take the advice of Henry and go by the river? What about his horses, Ebony and the blue roan of Otter's? What about Wolf? How long would it take, and when would he come back? Where would Ezra and Dove be then?

He sat down on a large flat rock at the river's edge, mindlessly watching the reflection of light from the rippling water, all the thoughts spinning in his mind, nothing getting settled, just more questions rising. Footsteps stirred the grass behind him, and he twisted around to watch Ezra approach.

"Takin' a moment alone, are ya?" asked Ezra.

Gabe dropped his eyes and tossed a pebble into the water, watched the splash get carried away with the current, then looked back at his friend. "Sort of, been thinkin' a lot, rememberin' and tryin' to forget all at the same time."

Ezra offered no comment, but sat near his friend, tossed a pebble of his own and waited for his friend to talk. The two sat silent for a spell until Ezra said, "It looks to me like it's more than just memories that's got you goin' silent."

Gabe sat quiet for a moment, then looked to his friend, "Been thinkin' 'bout family. Seein' Owl and his family makes me think about what me'n Otter wanted, and also about my sister, Gwyneth."

"Thought so. What'chu thinkin' 'bout doin'?"

Gabe sighed heavily, turned toward Ezra, "Thinkin' 'bout goin' to St. Louis. Those letters we sent with them trappers, one of 'em was to the attorney that was to take care of my father's estate. I told him to transfer everything to the bank in St. Louis. Thought about checkin' on that, maybe seein' if there's a letter from Gwyneth. She might be needin' some help," he shook his head and continued, "She just keeps comin' to mind. You know how it is when down deep you feel there's somethin' or somebody in need of your help. She's the only family I got left," and he grinned as he looked at Ezra, "'Ceptin' you, of course."

Ezra chuckled, "And Dove, and your nephew."

Gabe frowned, "What? My nephew? What . . ." he looked at the grinning Ezra, and as realization dawned, a smile painted his face and he continued, "You mean . . .?"

"Ummhmmm, yup. That's exactly what I mean,"

answered the broad grinning Ezra.

Gabe extended his hand, smiling broadly and said, "Well, congratulations old man!"

"Old man?! Just because I'm gonna be a father doesn't make me an old man!"

"It will soon enough!" chuckled Gabe. It was the first time in many days that he felt true joy in his heart. He slowly shook his head, looked at Ezra, "Then you won't want to be goin' to St. Louis then, will you?"

Ezra shook his head, "Dove's been talkin' to Yellow Bird, seems like the two of them done picked up where Otter left off, like sisters they are, and Bird said she doesn't want Dove leaving the village. She says she done talked to the chief and the elders, seems they would like all of us to stay the winter with 'em."

Gabe looked at his friend, stunned, "Even after that set-to with Moon Walker? They still want us to stay?"

"Truth of the matter is, you solved a purty big problem for 'em. Seems none of the elders were happy to see Walker return, none of 'em liked him or trusted him. That's why it didn't take much convincin' for you to deal with him. So now, they see you and me as *mighty warriors* that would be a grand addition to their village." He grinned as he watched Gabe's reaction. He continued, "After all, they're Shoshone and Dove is Shoshone, so that makes us *almost* Shoshone!"

"If that don't beat all. Just when you think you got folks figgered out, they up and surprise you." He looked at Ezra, "That might make it easier for me to go to St. Louis. You and Dove would have people to stay with, she'd have Bird around to help with the birthin', and you'd be here to take care of Ebony and the roan."

Ezra frowned, "What'chu mean, take care of Ebony and the roan? What're you gonna do, *walk* to St. Louis?"

Gabe chuckled, "No, the trader, Henry, he has a canoe that'd do to take me downriver. He said it'd be easier and faster taking the river. Safer, too."

"So you were already talkin' to him about goin'?" asked Ezra, incredulous to think his friend talked to a stranger about his plans first.

"No, I asked him about St. Louis, and he said, 'If you were to go. . .' and offered the canoe. Seems they're going northwest to find a river that'll take 'em to the ocean and don't wanna pack a canoe overland."

Ezra slowly lifted his head, looking at his friend, and understood. "*If* you go, when will you be back?"

"Probably late spring. By the time I get there, winter'll be comin' on, so if I left early spring, should get here in a couple months or so. Spring comes early in the low country, if you remember."

"Ummhmmm," replied Ezra, pondering. "That'd be 'bout the time the young'un should arrive."

The men sat silent together, watching the river, thinking, remembering and dreading as well as dreaming about what the days ahead might hold for them. They had been together and inseparable most of their lives, and now they might go to different parts of different worlds. Their friendship may demand they even move mountains to rejoin one another, but the efforts and intentions of even the best of men can often be overcome by the forces of time and distance. Neither man knew what might come upon them, but both were certain their friendship, brotherhood, and trust were all powerful forces and if the Lord wills, they would be together again come green-up in the mountains.

Gabe was the first to rise, offered a hand to his friend, and the two men walked back to the hide lodge where their friends and family waited. Gabe's mind was already rushing about and organizing what he would need to take, what could be left behind, and what time it would take to prepare. There would be much to do, and not the least of it would be go to Holder of Badgers and tell of his plans. His mind continued its race to organize and plan until they came to the lodge, then the greetings and conversations with friends became paramount.

31 / Arrangements

With so much water in the valley of the three forks, Dove had little difficulty finding a nest of duck eggs and when she surprised the men with eggs fried in bear fat with biscuit root and camas cakes, she was pleased with their delight. The men savored the rare treat, washed it down with big cups of steaming coffee, and were immediately put to work by Dove. She directed them as they took down the hide lodge, folded it up and put it on the travois behind the calm-standing grulla packhorse. They were moving the lodge to the village where they would place it near the tipi of Yellow Bird and her family.

"I'm goin' to talk to Henry, he said they'd be leavin' soon. So, I better talk to him about that canoe." Gabe was speaking to Ezra, but Dove overheard and asked, "What canoe?"

Ezra glanced at Gabe, then back at Dove and said,

"Uh, let's sit down and talk."

Gabe nodded, and walked away to go to the trader. Within moments, he approached the wall tent to see Alexander Henry and his partner, David Thompson, busy packing things up. Three other men were starting to take the tents down and another had gone to fetch the horses. Henry waved when he saw Gabe approaching, then stood up and came toward him to shake his hand, "So, made up your mind have you?"

"I think so. Seems to be the thing I oughta be doin'. Got some business in St. Louis and such, so, how 'bout we look at that canoe?" Henry grinned and motioned for Gabe to follow him around the wall tent. Behind the tent was a stack of packs, bundles, and sitting atop the stack was the canoe.

Gabe frowned, stepped closer and ran his hand along the sides of the canoe, and at the motion of Henry, the men flipped it over, so it sat upright on the grass beside the stack of goods. Gabe scowled as he looked at the craft, then looked at Henry, "I've never seen a canoe like this, where'd you get it?"

Henry grinned, "That came from the Kootenai. This is what they call a sturgeon-nosed canoe, cuz of the shape of the prow and stern." He pointed at the unusual shape of the craft.

"Well, the birch bark looks familiar, but the ends, that's different. I've seen the birchbark canoes of the Shawnee and the Ojibwe, with the prow that is rounded and comes up high to keep out the water, but that? That looks more like an alligator!" proclaimed Gabe.

Henry chuckled, "Lift it, see what you think," as he nodded toward the canoe.

Gabe reached down to grab one of the ribs and a thwart, lifted, and was surprised at how little the craft weighed. Even though it was about twelve feet long and almost three feet wide, he could easily pick it up by himself. He sat it down and began to examine the structure. With a skeleton of willow branches as ribs and the frame, the lower part was constructed of the inner bark of pine, sewn to the ribs with cedar root, and the gunwales of birch bark, also sewn with cedar root. It was a sturdy craft and he questioned, "How does it handle?"

"Very well. With the prow and stern with that elongated shape and covered like it is, it cuts through the water and any moss, weeds, or such like, and it knifes through rapids and moves smoothly on slow water. It's the best canoe I've ever handled," explained the trader.

"It looks like it would hold all my gear, and then some."

"It can carry four to six men and their gear, so you shouldn't have any difficulty."

"Well, sounds like we've got a deal," proclaimed Gabe, grinning. He stretched out his hand to Henry and was surprised when Henry said, "More'n that. I'm giving you the canoe! I can't take it, don't want to just leave it, and if you take it, then maybe someday down the line, you can return the favor!" Gabe grinned and the men shook hands. As they parted, each wished the other a safe journey and Godspeed.

When he returned to camp, all that remained was a stack of his gear and a tethered Ebony. He shook his head, grinning, and saddled up the stallion, loaded the rest of his gear and started for the village. When he arrived, the others were busy erecting the hide lodge, and he joined in, laying the poles in the cradle of the tripod. The three men hoisted the hide covering, but the women positioned it and stitched it together with the willow pins. The men stepped back and at Owl's urging, decided to visit with Holder of Badgers, the chief.

Owl led the way and the three were readily welcomed by the chief and his woman, Running Deer. She was busy at the cookfire and the chief was semi-reclined on a willow backrest between the cookfire and the lodge. As the others neared, he did not rise, but lifted his hand and greeted them, "You are welcome at my fire. Sit."

Owl seated himself closest to the chief, Ezra and Gabe back a little, but all near enough to converse freely. Badgers looked from Ezra to Gabe and said, "Owl tells me you will stay in our village for the cold season, that is good."

Owl replied first, "Spirit Bear will leave soon, but Black Buffalo and his woman will stay."

Badgers looked at Gabe with a frown, "You do not want to stay in our village?"

Gabe shook his head, "I must go back to the land of the white men for a time, but I will return. There are things I must do."

The chief nodded, looked beyond the men to see Two Moons, the shaman coming toward them. He motioned to the man to join them, which he did and seated himself near Ezra. He looked at the chief, then back at Ezra, "I am told you are a shaman among your people, and you can see beyond our time."

Ezra shook his head, "Musta been my woman talkin' to Yellow Bird." He looked at Two Moons and answered, "Among my people, we do not have shamans like your people. However, there are times that, well, I know things that others don't. But it's not something I can just do whenever I want to, it just happens."

The shaman and the chief looked at one another and Two Moons added, "I am also told you know of plants and more to heal."

"Some, but I would like to learn from you. I believe you know more of that than do I."

The shaman grinned, nodded, and looked to the chief with an expression that told of a mutual under-standing. Gabe caught the look, glanced at Ezra and knew his friend also understood. Gabe knew that with this understanding between the shaman and Ezra, and with his already displayed fighting skills, Ezra would have a prominent place among these people.

The chief looked at Gabe, "Do you leave soon?"

"At first light."

"We will look for your return. Until you do, always know you will have a place with my people. The Shoshone are known and there are many of our people and many villages. Should anyone question you, let them know that Holder of Badgers is your friend and will always be your friend. When you fought with the man who was the war leader, it was a good thing that you did."

"But chief, I didn't kill him. That hawk was not mine," protested Gabe.

"I know who threw the tomahawk. Our warrior, Black Owl, did that as he should. But it was you that fought and defeated the war leader, and for that, my people are grateful to you."

Gabe dropped his eyes, knowing there was little else he could say, but the memory of the one known as Moon Walker, and what he had done, was forever burnt into his memory. He sighed heavily, looked around, then to Ezra, "I think Dove might be fixing our meal."

Ezra grinned and each man reached forward to clasp forearms with the chief and the shaman, then stood and turned to leave. Gabe turned back and added, "I consider you and your people as my people. You are a great chief and I look to the time when I will return."

The chief nodded, and the three friends started to the newly erected hide lodge of Grey Dove. Gabe had been right, even with all the work of readying the lodge, Dove and Bird had worked together, and a hearty meal was simmering on the coals. Bird was pleased to use her new Dutch oven as Dove showed her and the biscuits made from the flour of the powdered roots of the biscuit root plant turned out as an exceptional treat for everyone.

Even though the thought of Gabe's expected departure hung over the group, the conversation was light and enjoyable as each time together seemed to draw the group into more of an extended family than just new friends. They talked well into the evening, enjoying the starlit night and the warm fire and the camaraderie, something that had been missing from the group for some time. When Gabe excused himself, he took Wolf with him for a walk in the moonlight as he spent some time with his Maker.

32 / Separation

Wolf lay beside Gabe as the man spoke to his Maker. Gabe glanced down at the complacent animal that lay with his muzzle between his paws, his eyes lifting now and then to watch Gabe. He reached down and ran his fingers through the scruff of his neck, noticing the mood of the wolf and believing he thought something new was in the wind. That is the way it is when animals are close akin to people, they have this innate ability to sense change and troubled spirits, and yet they always remain close and loyal. Every time Gabe looked at Wolf he was reminded of the closeness shared between Wolf and Otter, even though it was Gabe that found the pup in the cavern behind their cabin in the Wind River mountains. Gabe grinned at the remembrance, then stood, "Well boy," he stretched as the pink tinted the eastern sky, pushing aside the greys, "we better start getting stuff ready. Got a long ways to go and no tellin' how long its gonna take."

He stood for a moment looking down at the village, tipis with poles scratching the morning sky, wisps of smoke from early cook fires spiraling into the stillness of that time between darkness and light, dogs waking and stretching, men making their morning journey to the bushes, and the women stirring the coals and readying the morning meal. The village sat quietly between the line of rounded buttes and the snake like river at the edge of the wide valley. It was a serene image and Gabe wanted to brand it into his memory to carry with him on his journey. He grinned and with Wolf at his side, he started down the slope toward the hide lodge of Dove and Ezra.

Ezra came from a different butte and the men met as they entered the village, looked to one another, grinned, but said nothing as they walked together. Then as they neared the lodge, Ezra grinned, "I can smell the coffee already! That woman is a wonder, she is!"

Gabe chuckled, "And don't you forget it! If I ever find out you mistreat her, I'll have to turn you over my knee and paddle your behind like a spoiled step-child!"

Ezra stopped, looked at Gabe, let a smile paint his face, "You'd have to catch me first!" and turned to take off at a run. The two raced through the village, laughing, and slapping at one another, until they came to the cook fire of Dove, then slid to a stop, bent to put hands on knees and laughed. Gabe straightened up, "We ain't done that since we ran through the woods behind your daddy's church!"

"And then it was 'cuz he was chasin' us! Just cuz we let a squirrel loose in the church house!"

Both laughed at the memory and Dove stood, hands on hips, shaking her head. She pointed to the coffee as she returned to the lodge for other fixins for the meal. When she returned, the men were sitting, grinning, and staring at the flames as they sipped on their steaming coffee.

Although they dawdled over their breakfast, it was finished all too soon and Gabe stood to go to fetch Ebony from the herd at the edge of the camp. As he neared, he whistled his usual call, saw Ebony's head come up, and the stallion start prancing toward him, head high, tail and mane flying in the wind. The big black nuzzled Gabe and he rubbed the stallion's face and neck, looking him in the eye and speaking softly, "I'm sure gonna miss you boy." Gabe looked toward the herd and back at Ebony, "But I reckon you've got yourself a bunch of girlfriends that are gonna like your company, and if I know you, you're lookin' forward to spending time with them." He rubbed the horse's face as the stallion tossed his head up and down, then Gabe threw a strip of rawhide over his neck and led his long-legged friend back to the lodge.

Ezra had brought out Gabe's gear and stood watching as he came close, "I figger that by the time you get back, there's gonna be a bunch of black colts in that herd," nodding toward the distant horses.

"You're probably right about that, but you need to ride him ever now and then just to keep his manners in mind."

"Oh, I will. Course, both the women were taken with that horse and I wouldn't be surprised to see Dove sittin' atop him once in a while."

Gabe grinned at the thought as the swung the saddle onto the blanket on Ebony's back. He reached under the black's belly, grabbed the latigo and fastened the girth, giving the horse a bump with his knee to make him let the air out of his lungs, a trick the stallion occasionally used that would leave the girth loose around his middle. When Ebony bent his head around to try to nuzzle his master with the big lips, Gabe twisted to the side and chastised the horse with, "Don't you do that! I'll tighten this girth till you can't hardly breathe!" knowing all the while the black was playing with him.

Ezra had fetched his bay and saddled him, went into the lodge and brought out a bundle to lay across his rump, tied it down and stood waiting as Gabe finished tying off his gear. Dove came from the tipi and stood waiting until Gabe went to her and wrapped his arms around her, pulling her close into a bear-hug. He pushed her back to arm's length, "Now, you take care of that fella there," nodding toward Ezra, and with a glance to her waist, "and when I come back, I expect to see a fine, healthy, boy!"

Dove smiled, dropped her eyes and nodded as she dabbed at the tears that threatened to paint her face. She looked up at Gabe, "We will not follow you this time.

So, you must take care of yourself. You are our family!"

"Oh, I'll be back before you know it!" declared Gabe as he turned to mount up. But he was stopped by a call from the nearby lodge and he turned to see Yellow Bird and the two boys coming his way. The boys broke into a run and Gabe bent down to catch them in his arms. He hugged the two boys together, looked at them, "I expect you two to be proven warriors when I return! And you are to keep your family and my family safe while I am gone. Can you do that?"

Both boys grinned and chimed together, "Yes, we will!"

Bird came close and with arms outspread, walked into Gabe's embrace and hugged her new friend. Gabe looked around for Owl, but it wasn't until he heard the approach of a horse that he turned to see the stoic warrior sitting his mount beside Ezra, waiting for Gabe. Gabe grinned, looked at each of the women and the boys, nodded, and mounted up to join the two men. With a wave and a nod, they left the village and started for the confluence of the rivers where the canoe was stashed and waiting.

The men rode silently, each with his own thoughts, yet as men are wont to do, saying nothing, but letting their presence speak for them. Wolf trotted beside Ebony, matching stride for stride. They reined up and stepped down, and Gabe lifted the long and slightly cumbersome canoe just as Ezra grabbed at the stern to assist. They walked the canoe to the water and Gabe slid it into the

ripples, keeping the prow on the sand and using an at-
tached rawhide thong to secure it to a large stone. Ezra
looked at the craft, "I thought you said you had a canoe!
That shore don't look like any canoe I ever saw!"

Owl chuckled, "That is a Kootenai canoe. I have
seen them before. Very good canoe."

"But, what's with the nose and tail on that thing? It
sticks out like the nose of an alligator!" declared Ezra.

Gabe chuckled, but Owl frowned, "Alli . . . what?"

"Alligator!" answered Ezra, then seeing the con-
sternation on the face of Owl he added, "Oh, you've
probably never seen one! Let me see, well, . . ." he
looked at Gabe, "You tell him!"

Gabe chuckled as he put his saddle into the boat.
He dropped the blanket atop the saddle to cover the
holstered pistols and bow and rifle in the scabbard.
He turned to Owl and said, "Where we come from,"
then looked at Ezra, "well, not exactly where we come
from, but well south of our homes, in the swamps and
places like that, there are animals that," he paused,
trying to come up with words to describe such a
beast, then continued, "well, they have scales like a
snake, but they are great big." He turned toward the
boat, "Almost as big as that canoe! And they live in
the water, have real long tails, but their snout is like,"
he put his two hands together like a duck bill, "this."
He slapped his hands together, "Kinda like the end of
the boat. But their mouth opens, and they have lots of

teeth and they are big enough to eat a man!"

Owl looked from Gabe to Ezra to try to determine if they were speaking truth, then let a slow smile split his face and started laughing, shaking his head at the two men. Ezra looked at Gabe and the two men knew there was no way they could make Owl understand about alligators, so they just joined in the laughter.

Ezra took the large bundle from behind his saddle and dropped it into the stern of the boat. He looked to Gabe, "Otter worked hard on that. She wanted it to be a winter coat for you, but I reckon you can use it as you please. That's the grizzly you killed."

Gabe handed Ebony's reins to his friend, patted the horse on the neck, put his forehead on the face of the stallion and said, "I'm gonna miss you buddy. But I will be back for you." He turned to Ezra, started to clasp forearms, but the man pulled him into a bear hug and the friends held one another for an extended moment. As they parted, Gabe stretched his hand toward Owl who also pulled him into a hug. As the men stepped back from one another, tears welled up in the eyes of Gabe and Ezra, but Gabe quickly turned away and started to the canoe. He turned back to Ezra, "Push me off, will ya?"

Gabe stepped in, seated himself and picked up one of the two paddles, turned back to look at Ezra and was surprised when Wolf jumped in behind him. Gabe looked at the wolf, shook his head, looked at Ezra, "Guess he's comin' along!"

Ezra grinned, pushed the canoe further into the water, feeling it whisper across the sand, and once in the edge of the current, saw Gabe dip a paddle into the water. The men looked at one another, Gabe lifted the paddle in a wave, then turned to his task. Ezra stood with Owl watching his friend move away. Another wave, and Gabe dipped the paddle to push into the current. Wolf settled onto the loose grass that padded the bottom but watched with wary eyes as the canoe began to move with the current. Ezra lifted a hand to wave, but Gabe soon disappeared into the canyon of the Missouri. Ezra looked at Owl, "Guess he'll be ridin' the river for a spell!" and the two men mounted up to return to their lodges and their families.

Gabe felt a heaviness in his chest as his friends disappeared around the bend of the river. He knew he would be alone, except for Wolf and the thought of the big beast behind him brought a smile of comfort to his face, but perhaps the time alone would help him heal from his loss. He looked downstream of the wide river, saw a new and different terrain, and knew he was bound to ride the river for many days before he would make St. Louis, *if* he made St. Louis. But he knew no man was guaranteed a tomorrow, yet he was willing to put himself into the hands of his God and lean on the promise of Proverbs 3:5-6 *Trust in the Lord with all thine heart; and lean not unto thine own understanding. In all thy ways acknowledge him, and he shall direct thy paths.*

A Look at: Riding The River
(Stonecroft Saga 7)

B.N. RUNDELL KEEPS YOU COMING BACK FOR MORE IN BOOK SEVEN OF THE FAST-MOVING STONECRAFT SAGA.

The past always has a way of raising its ugly head and bringing havoc and heartache upon the unsuspecting. After spending most of five years in the Rocky Mountains, Gabriel Stonecroft finds it necessary to return to civilization to settle some long past accounts. He sets out from the headwaters of the Missouri River, with his only companion a wolf, navigating the wild river through the lands of the Blackfoot, Gros Ventre, Assiniboine and more. But an attack by a renegade French voyageur and his rebel Blackfoot companions is just one of the obstacles in his way.

Once he lands at the confluence of the Missouri and Mississippi the conspiring and deceitful ways of civilization weigh heavy upon him and his undertakes his duty to the memory of his father and his fortune. But subterfuge and betrayal rise to the fore in the form of a wicked banker and his sent-for bounty hunters, and Gabe, to protect his new friends, has to face the bringers of vengeance alone, on unfamiliar ground, in an inhospitable town, the fledgling St. Louis. Gabe's friendship with the early settler and trader from his first stay with the Osage, the man Auguste Choteau, brings a purpose and plan for the return to the river and the mountains of the west.

AVAILABLE JULY 2020 FROM B.N. RUNDELL AND WOLFPACK PUBLISHING

ABOUT THE AUTHOR

Born and raised in Colorado into a family of ranchers and cowboys, B.N. Rundell is the youngest of seven sons. Juggling bull riding, skiing, and high school, graduation was a launching pad for a hitch in the Army Paratroopers. After the army, he finished his college education in Springfield, MO, and together with his wife and growing family, entered the ministry as a Baptist preacher.

Together, B.N. and Dawn raised four girls that are now married and have made them proud grandparents. With many years as a successful pastor and educator, he retired from the ministry and followed in the footsteps of his entrepreneurial father and started a successful insurance agency, which is now in the hands of his trusted nephew. He has also been a successful audiobook narrator and has recorded many books for several award-winning authors. Now finally realizing his life-long dream, B.N. has turned his efforts to writing a variety of books, from children's picture books and young adult adventure books, to the historical fiction and western genres.

Made in the USA
San Bernardino, CA
08 June 2020

72962349R00175